IN THE BEGINNING

A NIC WARD COLLECTION

Z.J. CANNON

CONTENTS

HIGHER JUSTICE

If the sticky rings on the bar and the thick film on the windows were anything to go by, this place hadn't gotten a good cleaning in at least two decades. Probably around the same time most of its regulars had peaked. Now they looked like they weren't in any better shape than their chosen watering hole. They sagged on their stools, wiping greasy fingers on rumpled clothes, looking down at their drinks with the flat, dead eyes of people who had stared into the abyss and seen themselves staring back.

The music playing on the speakers was from thirty years ago, the high-school glory days of most of the people here. Or maybe I should say it was playing on the speaker, singular. The left speaker had cut out entirely, and the one on the right was well on its way. The music sounded as tired and faded as the regulars looked.

The man to my left stank of beer and desperation, just like

the rest of the place. The man to my right, though, smelled like expensive cologne, the kind that was basically bottled money and sex. He wore a tailored suit, with the tie loosened just enough to keep him from looking like a stuffed shirt.

He watched the other patrons hungrily. He had a drink in front of him, something dark and cloudy, but he hadn't so much as glanced at it for as long as I had been here. His fingers tapped lightly on the bar, but his face was patient. Like an angler who had cast his line and was willing to wait all day—or all night, as the case may be—for a nibble.

He didn't pay me any more attention than he did his drink. His gaze had drifted over me for a fraction of a second when I had first walked in, and he hadn't glanced my way again since. I must not have looked desperate enough for his purposes.

Appearances could be deceiving.

I turned to him and cleared my throat. "I hear you're the person to see if I want a job done."

It took a moment for the man to remember I existed. Slowly, he dragged his gaze to me, and blinked until his eyes came into focus. The irises were black—not the dark brown that people sometimes described as black, but pure obsidian, darker even than his pupils. The faintest hint of red flickered in their depths.

"That depends on the job," he said. "And the payment."

I lowered my voice and leaned closer. "I need someone dead." No sense in beating around the bush about it.

The man—although I supposed I shouldn't call him that, since he was no such thing—smiled. "There's no need to whisper. Nobody here cares enough to listen." He gave the bartender a cheery smile, and motioned him closer with a flick of his fingers. "Want to know something?" he asked in a voice loud enough to carry from one side of the room to the other. "This guy here is looking to have somebody killed." He jabbed a finger at me.

The bartender blinked. "You want another drink?" He asked, his gaze flicking first to my companion, then to me. When I shook my head, he shrugged and went back to smearing grease over a glass with a filthy rag.

But the people here weren't the eavesdroppers I was worried about. I was more concerned with the one who held my leash. I was off the clock for now, with Dennis asleep and alone. But all it would take was a single moment of wakefulness, or an intruder pushing open his bedroom door, and the mantle of my duty would return again. The keeper of my chains would know where I was, and that I wasn't with my charge. He would see everything I saw, and hear everything I heard—and everything I said.

Maybe I would get lucky and he wouldn't be paying attention. He had a lot to keep him occupied, after all. But I had learned, over the centuries, that it was never smart to rely on luck.

I kept my voice low. "Can you do it?"

The demon in front of me smiled. "The real question is whether you want me to. Do you know what I am, and what price I'll ask? A human assassin would cost you a lot less."

"This will take more than a human," I said. "The target has a guardian angel."

The demon whistled under his breath. "Then he must be in good with the man upstairs. That means big trouble for me if I get caught. Do you have any idea what those angelic types can do to my kind?"

I gave a short nod. "I've seen it up close and personal."

"Then you know that's not a risk any of us takes lightly. One lucky strike from one of those angelic swords of theirs, and..." He snapped his fingers. "Wiped out of existence, just like that." He shook his head. "Don't get me wrong, Hell isn't exactly a bed of roses. But I've worked my way up. Brought in enough human souls to earn myself some respect. It's a good life. And I'm not willing to risk being erased from the board for one more measly soul. Not when any one of these sad sacks would hand theirs over for the price of a good job or a beautiful wife. Or even an ugly wife." He laughed.

I didn't return the laugh. "I'm not offering you a soul."

"In that case, we have even less to talk about." He turned his back to me.

"I'm offering you something better," I said to the back of his head. "An angel feather."

He whipped around so quickly his elbow caught the edge of his glass. Dark liquid sloshed over the side. He took a deep breath and schooled his face to blank neutrality. But it was too late. I had seen the flash of hunger there.

Hell had no shortage of angels. At least not the fallen kind. But their wings had all been destroyed on impact, bones charred and broken, feathers burned to ash. And their descendants, the demons who had been born and raised there like the one in front of me, had never had wings at all. For how crowded the place was, there wasn't a single working set of angel wings in the place.

And angel wings were the only things that had the power to carry someone to Heaven.

Any demon with enough time and determination could hike their way to the mortal realm, like the one in front of me had. Getting into Heaven was another story.

Me, I didn't see why they'd want to. Heaven wasn't all it was cracked up to be. But the Fallen did love to tell stories about all they'd lost when they'd joined up with Lucifer's rebellion, and millennia of absence had blurred their memory of everything they'd been rebelling against in the first place. Demons like this one, who'd never known anything but the brutality of Hell and the dubious pleasures of this world, would do just about anything for a taste of the paradise they'd heard about at great-great-great-great-grandpa's knee.

It wasn't a matter of flying. It was something about the wings themselves. They were the only key that opened that divine lock. Someone who knew the trick of it could do it with a single feather. Which meant most demons would sell their left nut for the chance to get their hands on one. The last angel who had been sent down to Hell on one of the big guy's errands had never made it out. I heard a rumor that his body had appeared in a human morgue later, with broken shards of bone jutting out from his back, all that remained of his wings after the denizens of Hell had picked him clean. I didn't envy whoever had gotten the job of covering that one up.

The demon shook his head. "You're lying. Where are you going to get your hands on one of those?"

In answer, I let the disguise drop. For half a second, I was no longer a jowly middle-aged man in yesterday's clothes, indistinguishable from everyone else in the bar. Behind me, my wings unfurled. I glowed from within with divine light. It refracted off the glass in front of me, shooting tiny points of light out in every direction.

A few of the regulars cast startled glances toward me. But I had already faded back into the disguise. One by one, they shrugged and went back to their drinks. They had probably already written it off as an alcohol-induced hallucination.

I held out my hand to the demon. In my open palm rested a single feather. I had plucked it from my own wing. The spot where I had ripped it free still stung.

The demon stared at it without blinking. Slowly, he reached a hand out toward it.

I pulled my hand back, and closed my fingers over the feather. "On the other hand, maybe you don't want this. You've built a good life for yourself in Hell, after all."

With what looked like a great deal of effort, the demon brought his gaze up from my hand to my face. "That guardian angel you mentioned. That's you, isn't it?"

"Astute of you," I said. "Most people can't tell the difference between one angel and another at a glance. You had me pegged as a guardian in less than a second."

"A survival skill." He looked at me like I was a puzzle that needed solving. "Why, though? Why would you do something like this? Do you know what it will mean for you if your boss finds out? You'll end up down below with the rest of us."

I shuddered, and tried not to linger on the thought. "That's not something you need to worry about. The part that concerns you is that I'm good at what I do. So when you come after him, you need to make sure I don't see you. The mantle of a guardian angel..." I paused, searching for words, for a way to explain the sensation of the power settling over my body and using me however it saw fit. "I don't control it. I can't. I'm just the vehicle. If I see a threat to my charge, I won't be able to stop myself from doing whatever is necessary to protect him."

I knew. I had tried.

"You're asking a lot," said the demon. "I'm good, but I can't work miracles. That's the other side's department."

"Then maybe you don't want this after all." I tucked the feather into my pocket. "Not a problem. I'm sure I can find someone who does." I stood up, leaving my unfinished drink behind.

The demon stood fast enough that his stool almost toppled over. "Wait, wait. I'll do it. Just give me a name and a place, and a few days to prepare."

I squinted at the clock over the bar. Like everything else, it had accumulated a generous layer of grease and grime, which made it hard to make out the numbers. "You have eight hours."

"What? No. Not acceptable. I need more time than that. If you really need a rush job—which I don't recommend, if you want it done right—how does three days sound?"

I let the tip of the feather poke out of my pocket. Then I pushed it down again and strode to the door.

"All right, all right." He hurried after me. "Eight hours."

* * *

The next morning, I watched—as invisible as a ghost, and as powerless—as Dennis prepared for his latest one-on-one consultation.

He whistled during his short drive to the church. It had snowed about an inch overnight, and someone had shoveled the main walk. But they hadn't gotten around to the building out back, the one with the Carver City Homeless Outreach sign out front. Dennis didn't complain. He kept whistling as he dug out a shovel from the shed and cleared it himself. He sprinkled a layer of salt down for good measure, to melt the last patches of ice.

The building was small, only one room—or two, if you counted the basement. More than once, the church had suggested fundraising for an addition. But Dennis always smiled and insisted this was all he needed.

Once he was inside, he cleared a few stray papers off the desk. He pulled out a handful of books on choosing a career, and laid them out on the desk where the papers had been. He evicted a couple of stray dust bunnies with a feather duster. He poured two glasses of water and placed them precisely on the desk, one to his left hand, one to his right. To the one on the right, he added three drops from a small vial in the top drawer of his desk.

I did my best not to keep an eye out for the demon. But

any human will tell you how hard it is to force yourself not to think about something, and it's no different for us angels. I knew the demon was on his way—at least if he hadn't thought twice about the deal—which meant he was going to get me at my most vigilant.

But my sources had told me he was good. He chose easy prey out of laziness, not because it was his only option. I would simply have to hope my sources had been right.

I followed Dennis down the stairs as he descended to the basement. I wrapped my wings around him, covering his face, as if I could smother him that way. I placed my hands on his shoulders and imagined tightening them around his throat. But it could never be anything more than imagination. The guardian mantle wouldn't let me harm my charge. After thousands of years, and dozens of charges, this was the one lesson I had learned well.

The basement was small but cheerful, with pale yellow paint and the smell of pine from a plug-in air freshener. The air freshener did a good job of covering up any other smells that might otherwise have lingered. But I didn't think the paint and the pine scent were responsible for the way Dennis's mood always lifted when he came down here.

His whistling grew louder and more cheerful as he unfolded fresh plastic sheeting and laid it out on the concrete floor. He opened his toolbox next. He laid his tools out one by one along the edges of the plastic, caressing them lovingly as he did.

Jesus might have been a carpenter, but he wouldn't have recognized anything in Dennis's toolbox. There was nothing in there that could be used for building. Dennis was more interested in destruction.

His preparations complete, Dennis walked back up the stairs—just in time for a knock on the door. I checked the clock. Nine on the dot. I had hoped she would oversleep, or not be able to find a ride. But keeping this appointment must have meant a lot to her, because here she was, not even thirty seconds late.

I still saw no sign of the demon. Although I supposed that was a good thing. If I saw him before he got the job done, that would mean it was too late for both of us.

Dennis straightened the collar of his shirt and opened the door. He motioned his latest appointment inside. She looked just like all the others—long dark hair, big brown eyes that seemed to take up half her face. She couldn't be past her early twenties. She was thin past the point of attractiveness, more concentration-camp victim than runway model. Track marks dotted her arms.

But she had made painfully obvious efforts to clean herself up for the meeting. Her hair was freshly curled. Her sunflower-patterned dress, too thin for the weather, had to have been borrowed, judging by how it fit—too baggy in some places, too small in others.

"Thank you for meeting with me, Pastor Dennis," said the woman in a rough voice. I had seen her file, but I couldn't remember her name. After a while, they all started to blend together.

"No need to thank me," Dennis said with an easy smile. "It's what I'm here for." He motioned to the desk. "Why don't you take a seat, and we'll have a talk about your future."

She sat down in the chair opposite his. Hunger flared in her eyes as she ran her finger along the cover of one of the career books. They all had that same hunger, when they first sat down at his desk. And that same small, bright spark of hope, as they looked at what he was offering them and began to allow themselves to dream impossible dreams.

Carver City Homeless Outreach was Dennis's pet project. Under his direction, his church had opened a homeless shelter, which had grown to become the biggest in the state.

Mostly, Dennis took a hands-off approach. He kept the money flowing, and left the day-to-day work to the people he hired.

But every so often, he would stop by for a visit, and interview the people staying at the shelter. Nothing formal, just a chat. Enough to get a sense of their pasts, and their hopes and dreams. And then he would choose a candidate or two to meet with in person, and offer them one-on-one counseling to help them get back on their feet.

Dennis had specific criteria he used to select his candidates. As best I could tell, those criteria were that they had to be young, female, and attractive. And they had to have made enough of a mess of their lives that no one would think anything of it when they simply failed to return to the shelter one day.

Dennis sat down across from the woman. "Tell me, Marina," he said, leaning in toward her like she was the most important person in the universe, "if you could have anything, what would you choose? Don't be afraid to dream big. That's what we're here for."

Marina. Yes. That was her name. I remembered her from the shelter now. The one who had lost her children after her last fling with heroin. She was clean now, she had insisted. For good this time. Behind her back, the shelter workers had cast each other jaded looks, and placed bets on how long it would take before another needle found its way into her arm. Dennis had pretended he hadn't heard, but I had seen him listening.

Marina shook her head. "I... I don't even know. It used to be that I couldn't think beyond getting my kids back. Now it's hard to imagine even that much."

I didn't know why she was having such a hard time answering. The details might have differed, but deep down, all our desires—whether human, demon, or angel—came down to the same two things. Freedom. And justice.

"It's all right," said Dennis. "There's no need to answer right away. We'll take it slow. For now, why don't you make yourself at home? Take off your coat. Have a drink of water."

He pushed the water across the table to her. The one on the right. He always put the tainted one on the right. Every time, I wished he would make a mistake. But Dennis was a man who paid attention to the small details.

I wrapped my hands around his neck, and wished I could squeeze. His pulse pounded against my fingers, quick and eager. He tilted his head up and let out a long, slow breath of satisfaction. As if he could feel me there. As if he knew he was under God's protection.

Marina took a long drink of the water. She made a face. She peered into the glass and frowned.

Maybe she would listen to her instincts, and run. None of the others had, but she could be the first. If she left now, she might be able to get far enough away before it took effect.

Instead, she looked down at that career book again. She set the glass down with a shrug.

Dennis wasn't looking at her like she was the center of the universe anymore. He didn't need to. He stared over her head, watching the clock. Counting seconds. Marking time.

Marina didn't seem to notice. "Just the fact that you asked to meet with me gives me hope." Her voice was already sounding a little slurred. "Everyone has written me off for so long. I was starting to believe everything they said about me. But when you looked at me, you saw something more." She blinked, and blinked again, trying to focus her eyes.

It still might not be too late. She didn't need to get far, as long as she made it to where somebody could see her. I crossed over to the other side of the desk, and squeezed her shoulder hard enough that it should have hurt. It would have hurt, if I hadn't been on duty, the guardian mantle rendering me invisible to human senses.

I screamed in her ear, even though I knew she couldn't hear me. "Run!" She didn't even flinch.

Dennis gave her a warm, paternal smile. "Do you want to know what I saw in you?" He leaned in toward her, and tilted her chin up with his finger. "A drug-addicted whore no one would miss."

Marina's defocused eyes widened. "What..."

That was as far as she got. Her head slumped forward. Dennis caught her before she hit the desk.

He lowered her head gently. Then he stood, and scooped her into his arms in a practiced motion. He was facing a window, but there was nothing furtive about his movements. He strode with confidence to the basement door, the smile never leaving his face.

And why shouldn't he be confident? He had God on his side.

If there were any justice in Heaven or earth, someone would have passed by the window right then. Some passerby would have found themselves drawn to the building, sensing that something was wrong.

But God cared nothing for justice. All he cared about was worship and praise to feed his oversized ego. The humans who gave him what he wanted, who showered him in songs of his greatness and glory, earned his protection. No matter what they got up to when they weren't singing.

In Heaven, it was the same. The angels who knelt the lowest before his throne, and spoke the sweetest words, got to laze about in Heaven with their golden harps and ceremonial swords. The rest of us? We got jobs like this.

Dennis started up his whistling again as he carried Marina down the basement stairs. He laid her down on the plastic sheeting with the greatest of care. She moaned softly, like she was having a bad dream.

He knelt and brushed her hair back from her face. "Hush now, it's all right," he murmured. "It will all be over soon."

He ran his hands over his tools, pausing first on one, then another. Trying to figure out what to break first. His smile grew unfocused as he lost himself in his dreams. His whistling lost its tune. His eyes drifted shut.

That wasn't like him. Normally, at this point in the process, his eyes were bright and eager, as the basement and his anticipation lent him a surge of energy.

He was savoring the moment, I told myself. Nothing to worry about. There were no threats here.

Dennis slumped forward. He barely thrust his hand out in time to keep himself from pitching forward on the concrete. He gave a choked gasp that turned into a wheeze.

He was overexcited, that was all. He had gone too long between victims, and let the hunger build up too much. It would pass.

I might have believed my own lies if I hadn't caught a hint of something on the air, underneath the scent of pine. A whiff of expensive cologne.

It always hurt when the power took control of me. I had once seen a human walk outside after a storm, and set his foot down on a live wire without seeing it. I imagined it had felt something like this.

Before I was consciously aware of it, I had drawn my sword of lightning out of the ether. I spun to face the source of the smell. My eyes locked on to the demon, who was nothing more than a wisp of smoke with a pair of obsidian eyes. That same smoke was pouring into Dennis's nose and mouth, choking him, turning his eyes glassy and his face red. All the things I had worked so hard not to see.

The demon froze as our eyes met. I didn't. The power that had me in its grip wouldn't let me. I drove the sword deep into his smoky form. His eyes went wide as he resolidified around the blade. In less than the span of a heartbeat, his body had returned, the same one he had worn in the bar.

Dennis doubled over coughing. He stood, shaking his head, brushing himself off. He looked around, like he was trying to get his bearings, and stared right through us without seeing either of us.

I—or the power controlling me—drove the sword deeper into the demon's gut. I had missed his heart, on account of him not having one at the time. But this would kill him all the same. It would just take a little longer.

"I told you not to let me see you," I growled as I twisted the blade.

Black blood gushed from the demon's mouth as he snarled at me. "I should have known better than to trust an angel." The words came out garbled and choked, punctuated by another thick mouthful of blood.

"It's not me." Another twist. "I didn't want this."

The demon chuckled wetly. "It's easy to think that, isn't it? But whose choice was it to stay and kiss the feet of the man upstairs? Whose choice was it to let him hang that mantle on you?" He shook his head slowly, almost pityingly. "You chose weakness. You chose cowardice. If you were strong—" He hacked out another gush of blood. "If you were strong, you would have chosen to Fall."

With another snarl, he shoved himself forward on the sword. His fingers elongated into knifelike black claws.

I pulled back just in time to avoid the swipe. With a wet sizzle, the sword pulled free. Another gush of black blood came with it. It dribbled down to stain the basement floor, but Dennis would never see it. The same magic that hid the two of us from him now would keep him forever oblivious to the demonic stain. Not that his basement wasn't already stained enough with evil.

Oblivious to the fight taking place mere inches from his

nose, he smiled down at his prisoner. It looked as though he had already recovered from his brief ordeal. All the time and planning that had gone into my attempt on his life, and this was what it had come to. A few seconds of fear for him, the death of a demon who deserved it less than he did, and a stain on his floor that he would never notice.

Dennis bent down and picked up a slim, curved knife. He ran a finger over the blade, and ran his eyes slowly over Marina's exposed skin. Searching for the exact right spot to begin.

I didn't want to see. I had watched the same scene play out too many times already. Fortunately, I had other things occupying my attention.

The demon and I circled each other. He was holding his guts in with one hand, but if he knew how bad the damage was, he didn't seem to care. His eyes shone with a wild light. He gave a rattling hiss as he held his other hand up, claws at the ready.

It made sense, in a way, that he would choose to fight rather than run. He had to know that if he ran, the guardian mantle would make me chase him. He knew, too, that he wouldn't survive another strike from the sword. And he was aware of what it would do to him. He must have decided that if he was going down either way, he might as well at least bring me down with him.

Which was hardly fair of him. He had known what it meant to go up against a guardian angel. I had warned him myself. There was no sense in him blaming me for it, when I wasn't in control of my own actions. If I were, I would turn around right now and drive my sword through Dennis's heart.

Weak. The demon's accusation drummed like a heartbeat against the inside of my skull. *You chose weakness. You chose cowardice. Weak. Weak. Weak.*

For the first time in my long existence, I reached for the mantle instead of fighting it. I lost myself in it, letting it drown out the demon's voice with its own. *Kill him,* urged the power thrumming through me. *Destroy the threat.*

And I would. I would obey; I would always obey. I had no choice.

I was weak. I always had been.

I would do what God required of me. I just had to wait for the right moment.

Our circles grew tighter and tenser. The demon slashed out with his claws again. The razor tips came inches from my heart.

Almost. Almost. *Now.*

Destroy the threat, the power inside me sang. And I sang along with it, a howl of triumph and helpless fury.

I drew the sword back—and ran it through the demon's heart.

His snarling fury turned to mute shock. But only for an instant, before his features melted into a blur of smoke and shadow. The rest of his body followed. Through his translucent form, I could make out the dark outlines of Dennis standing behind him and the unconscious Marina on the floor. The smoke lightened to a pale gray, then drifted away on a nonexistent breeze. The last thing to go were his eyes, dark and accusing.

Then they, too, melted into nothing, and he was gone.

Leaving me with a clear view of Dennis, directly behind him, impaled on my sword.

The sword had gone through his back, and come out through the center of his ribcage. He looked down at himself, and made a choked, disbelieving noise. I wondered what was going through his mind as he tried to make sense of what he was seeing—a hole in his chest, a blinding pain, and nothing visible to cause either one.

Then again, I didn't much care what he was thinking.

He slumped forward on the blade. The noises stopped. I shook him free, and stared down at his crumpled form, hardly able to believe my own triumph.

The moment the mantle had taken hold of me, I had known I wouldn't be able to stop it from doing its work. But as the demon and I had circled each other, his voice pulsing in my brain, it had occurred to me that maybe I didn't have to stop. Maybe all I had to do was outsmart it.

I had waited for the exact right moment, until the demon was directly in front of Dennis. Until the same strike would kill them both. Then I had zeroed in on the threat to Dennis's life with singular focus, letting the mantle's own power distract me from Dennis himself for the split second it had taken to run them both through.

The odds of it working had been one in a million. But then, I'd had nothing to lose.

I let the sword fall from my hand. I wouldn't be needing it anymore.

Marina was still unconscious, whimpering in her restless dreams. She would wake into a worse nightmare than whatever scenes were playing behind her eyes. I wanted to carry her out of here, and take her someplace safe. Dennis could no longer harm her body, but if she woke up here, even in death he would leave a scar on her soul. I would have spared her that if I could have.

But I already knew I wouldn't have time. A sound was growing all around me—a whispering hiss of flame.

There was only one place for an angel who defied Heaven.

The screams of the damned, as faint and eerie as the winter wind outside, howled through the room. Marina frowned and shifted restlessly.

A portal yawned open at my feet. Heat blasted my face. The whisper of the flames became a crackle and a roar. But when I looked down, all I could see was darkness.

Had this been what I was afraid of for so long? Was this the threat that had made me accept the power bestowed upon me, and use it to protect so many monsters in human skin? Down in that pit, at least the evil was out in the open. I could hear it in those screams, and in the hungry growls that followed. What I didn't hear was a single cheerful whistle.

I was weak. I always had been. But that would change. The Fall wouldn't kill me; the lake of fire would spit me into the rocky pits of Hell, as it had each of the Fallen before me— charred and flightless, but still alive. But it would burn the weakness from me first.

And to survive in Hell, I would need to become stronger still. It would harden me into what I needed to become. What I should have become long ago.

A guardian.

Like the demon in the bar, I intended to find more for myself in Hell then pain and suffering. But unlike him, I wouldn't satisfy myself with lurking in bars, ensnaring easy targets for the sake of whatever scraps the lords of Hell might toss me. I already had my thoughts set on higher things.

Heavenly things.

And I had an angel feather in my pocket.

I would let Hell forge me into someone worthy of my desires. And once it did, God himself wouldn't be safe from me.

I didn't wait for the portal to pull me in. I stared down into the black depths with a feral grin, and jumped.

There was no justice in Heaven or earth. But I would change that.

THE DIZZY FALL

The angel's body lay facedown on the floor of the church. From the look of it, he had hit his head on the edge of a pew on his way down. It had left a nasty gash across the side of his forehead, and a dark smear of blood down the wood. Angel blood, as it turned out, was red just like ours.

The head injury hadn't been what killed him, though. No, that honor went to the multiple stab wounds that had turned his torso into Swiss cheese. I counted at least six, and his blood-matted wings were probably hiding more. Someone really hadn't liked this guy. Not much of a surprise, really. Fighting on the side of the light tends to make you more enemies than friends. I would know.

A few feet away, a short, round priest paced in front of the altar, muttering and periodically crossing himself. My friend Declan stood at the edge of the puddle of blood, twisting his hands together. If *friend* was the right word for someone who hadn't bothered to visit me in prison, and whose contact with me since then had been limited to a Christmas card every year with a picture of his wife and smiling children inside. I never sent him one back. I wasn't the Christmas-card type.

"It isn't a..." Declan made a strange flapping gesture. It took me a minute to realize he was trying to mime wings. "Is it? Those things have to be fake." He reached out like he was going to touch the bloodstained feathers, but pulled his hand back at the last minute.

"You tell me. You're the cop." The words came out with a bitter edge.

He had the decency to flush pink at that. "I'm off duty," he said, as if that were an explanation. "I haven't called this in yet. This is my church; the priest knows I'm on the force. He called me in as a friend. He didn't know what else to do."

"And you called me."

"There are rumors about what you've been doing since you left the force. I never really took them seriously, of course, but..." He waved a hand helplessly toward the body, as if to say, *What else was I supposed to do?* Now that was a treat for the old ego. Nothing like being someone's last resort.

"What I've been doing since I got out of prison, you mean," I said flatly. Yep, answering Declan's phone call had been a mistake.

He stared down at his feet. "Some of us never believed you did it, you know."

"Funny, I must have missed you all speaking in my defense at the trial."

He flushed deeper this time. "I'm sorry."

As if an apology could erase the three years I had spent in that place. I took a deep breath. "It's in the past. Anyway, it worked out for the best. I was never cut out to be a cop. I'm happier now."

I could read his question on his face. *Happier doing what, exactly?* But he didn't ask, so I didn't answer. Not that I would have told him the truth either way.

"Let me take a closer look," I said instead. I walked in closer and crouched down to examine the body. There was blood on my shoes, but I didn't care. I had stepped in worse.

I lifted one of the wings—it was heavier than I expected—and examined it from all angles, just to confirm what I had already figured out. It wasn't a fake. These wings were a part of his body, as much as his arms or his legs. This was no mischief-maker celebrating Halloween three months late.

This was a first for me. I had seen plenty of demon corpses over the years. Even made a fair number of them myself. And dead humans? That went without saying.

But an angel... that was a new one. I didn't know what out there had the power to bring down one of the Heavenly Host. To be honest, I wasn't sure I wanted to know. But I had a bad feeling I was going to find out. Nothing said demonic activity quite like a dead angel, and shutting down hell's operations on earth was pretty much the extent of my job description. The second I had seen the body, I had turned my ringer up to max. The call from my boss would be coming any minute now.

Well, when that call came, the more information I had for him, the better. "Let's see who you are," I murmured. I grasped the angel's shoulder as gently as I could. I knew he couldn't feel it, but but touching an angel with my bare hands, alive or not, felt wrong on a deep level. Like washing my hands in the baptismal font. I didn't know what I expected—a bolt of lightning from above, maybe—but nothing happened. His body was as cold as any human corpse.

I flipped him over so I could get a look at his face. No

doubt the boss would want a description. His wings bent under him, and something snapped with a soft crack. I winced.

Then I forgot all about his wings as I got a good look at his face.

He had spent a good long time lying in a pool of his own blood, and a fair amount of it had congealed on his face. But the red wasn't enough to hide his identity from me.

It looked like I wasn't going to be getting that call from my boss today after all. Or ever again.

I must have made some kind of noise, because suddenly Declan was there, bending over me in the perfect position for me to flip him onto his back and maybe break a finger or two in the process. I restrained myself, even when he placed a hand on my shoulder as if he gave a shit about me.

"Are you okay?" he asked.

I wanted to tell him to screw off. Ten years of silence, and now he had the gall to ask for a favor? I was tempted to say just that. Or worse, tell him the truth: that I had no idea what to do.

I liked rules. Absolutes. It was one of the reasons I was good at what I did. Also the reason I had been such a terrible cop. Maybe I should have expected what I found inside the police force—the payoffs behind closed doors, the people on the ground ordered to look the other way where certain powerful interests were involved. Maybe I could have gone along if I had been a little less exacting, a little more willing to compromise. But I had come out of the womb this way, so really, it was fate that my police career had ended the way it had.

I had collected evidence, as slowly and methodically as I would have done for any other crime. And then I had gone to the top, above the heads of everyone involved. Or so I thought. The next day, my folder full of evidence was gone, never to resurface, and I was being framed for accepting bribes.

Bribes, of all things. More corruption. They should have made it murder instead. At least that would have given me a reputation I could have lived with.

Even then, I had trusted the system. Why would I have become a cop in the first place if I hadn't thought justice was real? I had hired a lawyer, and rejected the plea bargain they had offered me. I had gotten up on the stand and told the truth. I had thought that would be enough, right up until the judge banged the gavel and pronounced the guilty verdict.

I didn't believe in the justice system anymore. But I still believed in justice. I believed in rules, in procedures, in knowing what to do and doing it.

But there were no rules for finding my boss lying dead on the floor of a church, where everyone could see his true form.

I stood up and took another deep breath. "Go home," I ordered Declan. "You were never here. This is my case now."

* * *

The Inquisition found me when I was in prison. They liked my sense of justice. The fact that I had been written up for excessive force on two separate occasions also probably didn't hurt. My new bosses valued people who could get things done. And on the excessive-force thing, yeah, I know, I didn't exactly make it hard for my old bosses to frame me. That still didn't make it right.

The Inquisition gets a bad rap. Even back in the old days, the vast majority of what they found was genuine demonic activity. But nobody ever tells those stories, do they? A few sob stories about poor innocent burned witches, and now they have to operate in secret. Even most officials within the church don't know they're still around.

Which was why I couldn't answer the priest's questions about who I was and why Declan had called me. "I'm an old friend of Declan's," I repeated for the third time. The words tasted bitter in my mouth, but hey, if it got me what I needed to know. My investigative skills might have gone rusty over the past ten years, but I still remembered the fine art of telling civilians what they needed to hear.

My answer didn't seem to hold any more weight for the nervous priest then it had the first two times. He frowned. "And you've dealt with... these situations... before?"

"Many times," I assured him, not quite truthfully. I might not have encountered a dead angel before now—let alone my own boss—but when it came to the supernatural, he wasn't going to find anyone more qualified.

"Then this is a common occurrence? Oh dear, oh dear." He crossed himself again and muttered a prayer.

I switched gears before the priest could start pacing again. "I'm trying to figure out what the..." Even talking to someone who should have had no problem believing in angels, it was hard to say the word. "What the deceased was doing here in the first place. Could he have been meeting with someone? Who else would have been here last night?"

"Just Father Andersen. He liked to keep the doors open well into the night, in case any lost souls were to wander in. He also liked the quiet, for reading the Bible and writing in his study. But meeting with an angel? My goodness. He was a pious man, to be sure, but no. He would have told me." His eyes widened. "Surely you're not... you don't think *he* did this?"

The possibility honestly hadn't occurred to me until just now. A human against an angel? There wasn't any question who would win that fight. Or so I would have thought. But if this Father Andersen had been the only other person here...

"Right now I can't rule anything out."

The priest shook his head vigorously. "No, no. Father Andersen was a man of the cloth. He would never raise a hand against a servant of the Almighty."

"If I wanted to talk to him, where could I find him?"

As if in answer, the priest held up a cell phone. The sight jarred me for a second; for some reason I always expected priests to be stuck in the medieval era, carting around a scroll and a quill pen. Hypocritical, I know, coming from an Inquisitor who had brought down demons with a machine gun more than once.

"I've been trying to call him since I found..." He wiggled his fingers toward the angel's body, then hastily averted his eyes and crossed himself again. "He hasn't answered yet. He's probably still asleep. That's not unusual for him at this hour, considering the late hours he keeps."

Asleep, or dead, or on the run. But I didn't mention those alternate possibilities. Either the priest had already thought of them, or he was better off for his ignorance. "Can you give me his number? His address, too."

With shaking fingers, he entered both into my phone. Mine was a more basic model than his. I didn't like it when people could get in touch with me too easily.

"Mind if I take a look in Father Andersen's study?" I asked, slipping the phone back into my pocket.

He looked like he didn't like the idea much. But what else was he going to do, with the blood of an angel staining the floorboards only a few feet away from us? I was the expert, and trusting me had to be less scary than the thought of me leaving him to figure this out all on his own. He slipped a key into my hand and pointed me down the hall. When I turned my back on him, he had already gone back to compulsively crossing himself and muttering frantic prayers.

Father Andersen's study had a homey smell, like books

and woodsy cologne. The first thing I noticed was the Bible on his desk. It was open to the very end, Revelation, with both facing pages slashed with yellow highlights. Not a reassuring sight, that. On the other hand, I'd read Revelation, and mostly what I got out of it was that religion and drug trips don't mix. The angel was a bad sign, I had to admit, but it wasn't a Sign with a capital S. The world wasn't going to end anytime soon; if history was any guide, it would keep on spinning and spinning, whatever any of us trapped on this ride had to say about it.

At least that was what I told myself.

Next to the Bible was a leather journal, also open. It sat at a skewed angle, with a pen lying across the page, like someone had interrupted him in the middle of his writing. I bent down to take a closer look. The handwriting was thin and wobbly, like it belonged to an old man. I had to squint at the page for a couple of minutes before I could decipher the letters.

It started in the middle of a sentence. The rest of the entry was probably on the previous page. *...no choice but to accept that what he tells me is true. I can no longer take refuge in denial. But I will not abandon my sacred calling, no matter how futile it may seem. I will do as he asks, and guide humanity through the coming darkness. I must, because there is no one else to—*

That was where it ended, with a line that ran all the way to the bottom of the page. Someone had startled him. The odds of him being home in bed, peacefully asleep, were looking dimmer by the minute.

I flipped backward through the journal. His penmanship got progressively steadier as I went back in time. He had written a lot about how Satan was testing him, and how he wouldn't let his faith be shaken. Standard stuff, I would have thought, if not for the evidence to the contrary back down the hall.

I kept waiting for him to explain what exactly these tests were, what it was that had left him so shaken. But every entry was maddeningly vague. Almost purposefully so, like he had been guarding against exactly this situation— someone poring over his words and trying to discover his secrets. Either that, or he had been afraid to voice the truth even to himself... whatever that truth was.

Who was this "he" who had left Father Andersen so disturbed? My boss, I thought at first—it had to be. But no priest would have mistaken an angel of God for a creature of Hell. Trust me, I've seen plenty of both. Not only that, but why would my boss have come to him in the first place? He didn't go around appearing to humans willy-nilly. Even when he needed to give us orders, he only met with us face-to-face when there was no other option. If he had business with some random local priest, he would have sent one of us.

Yes, even if that business wasn't the violent kind. We aren't one-trick ponies, you know. Even if fighting is what we're best at.

Finally, near the beginning of the book, I found what I was looking for. Or I thought I did. *I had a visitor today,* he had written in a thick scrawl that looked nothing like the shaky writing from his final entry. *Or I think I did. I'm still not entirely sure whether the entire incident was a dream. The man claimed to be—* But the sentence after that was scratched out so thoroughly I couldn't decipher a single one of the words. The next decipherable sentence read, *I prayed for aid, and divine guidance, but neither came,* which was no help at all.

I skimmed through a long and detailed explanation of the fear he had felt and where exactly in his body he had felt it. Despite myself, I started to yawn. But I snapped wide awake again when I hit a paragraph that started, *My visitor—I fear to call him by the name he gave me—said he was here to bring me news that would alter the shape of the world itself. He told me...*

But he had scratched out the rest of the sentence with even more energy than he had the earlier part. The pen had torn through the paper in places. I smoothed the page under my hands, and held it up to the light, but all I got from that was the certainty that I didn't have a chance of reconstructing what he had written.

I didn't throw the journal across the room. But it was a near thing. I mean, really? He had written out the answer plainly for me—after making me go through almost an entire journal's worth of his chicken scratch—only to yank it away at the last second? If I had been of a more paranoid bent, I might have thought he had done it just to mess with me. Or that *somebody* up there was messing with me, at least.

I raised a single finger—three guesses which one—and aimed it skyward. Then I sighed, lowered my hand, and murmured a brief, contrite prayer. It wasn't the Almighty's fault so many of his children seemed to live to make my life difficult. First the idiot teenager last week who had summoned a demon in his mother's basement, and now this.

I scanned the rest of the entry without much hope, and found pretty much what I expected to find—a big fat nothing. *I will not believe this blasphemy,* he had scrawled, his pen digging viciously into the paper. *I will remain strong in my faith.*

I snapped the journal closed. There was a row of identical journals on the bookshelf, and I flipped through them all. But the entries all had earlier dates on them, and they were all just notes on his Bible reading. The only useful bit of information I got from them was that he hadn't started studying Revelation until this visitor of his had shown up. Which, again, not reassuring.

And that was basically the extent of Father Andersen's

study. Journals. Bibles. Books on theology. Maybe cop me would have known where to go from here, but I hadn't done this kind of investigation in ten years. In the old days, a lot of the Inquisition's work had been investigative, but these days, by the time we got called in, the suspect was generally obvious and the verdict was clear. We were judge, jury, and executioner—but detectives, we were not. I was about to start searching for hidden floorboards—I was that desperate for a clue—when my phone rang.

I pulled it out of my pocket. Blocked number. I answered, but didn't say anything. That was usually enough to confuse the robocallers and make them hang up.

A smooth, bland voice started reading off a series of numbers.

"Who is this?" I interrupted. Those numbers were code for the location of an in-person meeting. But my boss was the only one who had the authority to do that. And my boss was lying cold and stiff in the other room. Besides, that voice wasn't his.

The voice paused briefly, which let me know there was a real person on the other end. After a couple of seconds, he started his recitation over from the beginning. I tore a page out of Father Andersen's journal and scribbled the numbers down with his pen.

When he stopped, I opened my mouth to repeat my question. But before I could speak, I heard a click. The caller had hung up.

I read the numbers over until I had memorized them, then tore the paper into confetti and threw it in the trash. It looked like I was going to get some answers after all. Which was a good thing, because all of a sudden I had a lot more questions.

* * *

The code told us where to meet. The numbers were different every time, but the format never varied. Latitude and longitude first. Then an address, ciphered.

At times, I thought it felt like overkill. But considering our enemy was *the* Enemy, capital E, I supposed there was no harm in being overly cautious. The devil, as they say, is in the details.

Today, it turned out we were meeting in a church basement that smelled of crayons and stale coffee. The others were already there, crammed into chairs too small for them. Crude children's drawings of Noah's Ark were tacked up all around. I felt out of place as soon as I walked in. Maybe it was just that I had never been comfortable around kids. Or maybe it had more to do with the rifle strapped to my back, the twin pistols at my belt, and the knives in my ankle sheaths.

We did have our own dedicated spaces, one or two on each continent. But we only used those for training, and for big gatherings, the kind that only happened once every few years or when something apocalyptic was going down. The rest of the time, we met up in smaller groups, and in places no one would think to look for us.

Usually that meant a church, because whether the people who came here every Sunday to sing hymns and drink that stale coffee knew it or not, we had as much right to this space as they did. Without us, their church and every other would have been wiped off the map a long time ago.

The dozen or so Inquisitors in the room were all faces I recognized. All the currently active Inquisitors in the state, the same ones I saw at every infrequent in-person briefing. Most of the time, we got our orders by phone. Just the fact that we were meeting face to face meant something was up. But I took some small amount of solace in the fact that we were sitting here in these kiddie chairs. If this were really a Book-of-Revelation situation, we would have been feeling our asses go numb from the stone chairs in one of the cavernous rooms deep under the Vatican.

Unless, of course, whoever had called us here had brought us here to kill us.

Which was why I had come armed for bear—armed for demon, really, but you'd be surprised at the similarities—and why I didn't sit down. I got several curious looks as I positioned myself just inside the door. Most of the time, we didn't come armed to these briefings. It wasn't a written requirement or anything, but it was a sign of respect—to each other, and to our boss. Breaking the taboo would have made me feel uneasy, if not for the smell of the angel's blood that still lingered in my nose.

I didn't know his name.

I didn't know why that occurred to me just then, or why it bothered me so much. He had been our boss, and we had been his tools, to use as he saw fit. He gave us our assignments, we carried them out. We'd never had more of a relationship with that. Speaking purely for myself, I'd never wanted one. Sure, angels were the good guys, but that didn't mean they weren't terrifying in their own right. I wasn't in any hurry to sit down and have a beer with one.

But now he was dead. Which I figured meant we were supposed to grieve. Only how could I grieve for someone who had only ever been a voice reading numbers over a telephone, and a pair of hands passing out lists of names? How was I supposed to remember someone whose name I didn't even know?

It shouldn't have bothered me the way it did. But once the thought occurred to me, I couldn't get it out of my head.

A skinny guy near the back of the room—Trenton, I thought his name was—spoke first. "Did you get a memo the rest of us missed?" he asked with an uneasy laugh, eyeing my gear.

"You could say that." When I had recognized the body in the church, I hadn't imagined this moment. I had always thought one of the benefits of not being a cop anymore was not having to give people news like this. "The boss is—"

"Here," finished a low, booming voice from the doorway.

I spun to see a man in full tactical gear stride into the room like he owned the place. I glanced at his eyes, and immediately looked away. Angels could wrap themselves in human disguises all they liked, but there was only so much they could do about their eyes. That heavenly fire was impossible to hide.

Everyone else shot confused looks at him, and at each other. Me, I found myself reaching for one of the pistols at my belt before I realized what I was doing. I dropped my hands to my sides, feeling ridiculous. I knew how to tell the difference between an ally and an enemy. This man wasn't one of the Fallen. He was on our side. And if anyone could be said to have the face of an angel, it was him. From his golden curls to his round cheeks to his clear blue eyes, he looked like he had stepped out of one of those soft-focus paintings of frolicking cherubs.

But when he looked at me, the hairs on the back of my neck stood on end.

He slammed the door shut behind him. As soon as it closed, he abandoned the human disguise. His shoulders broadened, and he grew so tall his head brushed the ceiling. His skin glowed alabaster white. His wings extended out in either direction, snowy feathers wreathed in white flame.

If the flames hadn't been enough of a hint, his face would have clued me in. I had seen that face every Sunday in the stained-glass window of my childhood church, squirming on a pew between my parents. All he was missing was the flaming sword.

They hadn't sent just any old angel to replace the boss. This was the Archangel Michael himself.

I might have fallen to my knees, if a phrase from my training hadn't come back to me at just the right moment. *An Inquisitor kneels to no one but God.* Instead, I picked my jaw up off the floor. I did my best to salvage my dignity by crossing my arms and leaning back, the picture of unimpressed. "What's going on?"

Michael's eyes rested on me for only a fraction of a second. That was more than enough. His regard washed over me like a bath of cold flame. I had to look down at myself afterward to make sure my body hadn't been charred to ash.

"As of three hours ago, I am your commanding officer." His voice hissed and crackled through the room like flame. I half-expected all those crayon drawings to burn up right then and there.

Isn't this a bit below your pay grade? I wanted to ask Michael. I didn't say anything.

Michael went on as if the interruption had never happened. "The Enemy caught us off guard, and struck a blow with the potential to undo everything we have ever fought for. All of Heaven is depending on you to contain the damage. I trust that you will fulfill your duties quickly and efficiently, and above all, discreetly." He swept his gaze over us again; I quickly averted my eyes. "More than you know depends on you now."

This had to be about more than our boss. His death alone couldn't be enough to shake Heaven this badly. But I had no doubt that this was connected to him—and to whatever had shaken Father Andersen so badly. I wanted to ask what was going on, but more than that, I wanted Michael's eyes never to land on me again. So I kept my mouth shut.

"The Enemy has suborned each of these individuals, and

plans to use them to further his plan. Eliminate them before he gets the chance." Michael reached into a satchel that hadn't been there a moment ago. He handed me a slim strip of parchment with a name in blocky typewriter print—*Graig Hornsby*. As soon as I read the name, the paper disintegrated to ash in my hands.

It looked like everyone else in the room was too cowed to ask any questions, same as me. Maybe, also like me, they were doing their best to take comfort in the familiar routine. Receive a target. Eliminate the target. Remove the threat, avert the apocalypse, and so on. Another day in the life.

I could tell from the looks in their eyes how badly they wanted to believe that. I wanted it, too. Maybe even more badly than they did. They hadn't seen the body in the church. I needed to know that nothing had changed, that my purpose remained the same. Because if I didn't have that...

A sudden wave of dizziness swept over me. For a second, I couldn't feel the ground under my feet. My body felt impossibly light; I wasn't sure I even existed. It reminded me of the day I had caught my mother smoking a cigarette out on the front porch when I was seven years old. When she had seen me watching her, she had stomped it out with a shrug and a sheepish smile. *You caught me.*

I had locked myself in my room and lain facedown on the pillow, still as a corpse. I had held my breath as long as I could, over and over, just to make the animal panic set in and remind me that I was still here. I had needed to feel real, now that nothing else did anymore. Now that the ultimate arbiter of rules had broken one herself, and the order that had held my small world together lay in ashes on the porch.

When I had come down for dinner hours later, pale and trembling, my mother had scowled at me. *Some children,* she had sniffed, *would show their parents a little grace.*

As the others silently read the names on their own slips

of parchment, a searing-hot hand came down on my shoulder. I jerked away before I could stop myself. When I looked down at where Michael had touched me, there was a blackened handprint burned into my jacket.

Michael leaned in toward me. I had to fight not to back up against the wall. *He's one of the good guys,* I reminded myself, as I did my best not to look him in the eye. *He's on our side.*

"I have one more instruction for you personally," he said, in a voice too low to be overheard. "You are to cease your investigation at once."

I blinked up at him, too startled to remember not to make eye contact. I hadn't said anything about the investigation.

"Our old boss," I said, and wished all over again that he had told us his name. "What happened to him? Who killed—"

Michael's hand came down on my other shoulder, harder this time. I fought back a scream as his fingers burned through my jacket and into my skin. "He is no longer your concern. Complete your assignment. Ask no questions. Heaven is watching."

Our old boss used to close every meeting that way. *Heaven is watching.* He had meant it as a benediction, a reminder that we were never alone out there as we fought the good fight. But in Michael's voice, it sounded like a threat.

* * *

The target was a priest. His house, a small cottage down a winding driveway behind a sprawling Catholic church, was my first clue. The cassock hanging neatly on a hanger inside his bedroom door was the second.

I thought back to the missing Father Andersen. *Ask no questions,* I reminded myself. It wasn't as if it was the first time I'd been sent after a servant of God who had fallen to the forces of darkness. Father Andersen had been convinced the Enemy had been trying to tempt him away from God. Maybe the Enemy had finally succeeded—and not just with Father Andersen, but this other priest too.

Maybe this was all as simple as that.

But there'd been nothing simple about the Archangel Michael showing up in that shabby church basement.

I took a deep breath and emptied my mind of everything but the image of the sacred flame that, to me, represented my holy purpose. I had joined the police force looking for that purpose. I'd found nothing but people bending the rules in their favor. Now, though, I enforced the laws of Heaven, and there was no bending those. The thought of those ultimate laws, a steel skeleton holding up the teetering skyscraper that was this world, straightened my back and calmed my breathing. The white flame in my mind steadied.

My fingers hovered over my pistols, but I passed them over and pulled out one of my consecrated knives instead. Even with the silencer, guns were too loud for a suburban neighborhood like this one. Michael had told us to make discretion a priority.

Michael. At the thought of him, my skin prickled with unease. I put the memory out of my mind and focused on the figure on the bed.

I tried to be as quiet as possible, but the floor creaked under me as I padded to his bed. Just my luck that the priest was a lousy sleeper—his eyes snapped open immediately. I gave an inward groan. Now there was going to be a fight.

That meant two possible outcomes, neither of which I needed tonight. Either he'd fight like an ordinary human, giving me an easy win and the prize of walking away with the guilt of having beaten someone who'd never stood a chance... or whichever demon had corrupted him had gifted him with some sort of supernatural power, and I would limp out of here nursing wounds I didn't dare go to the hospital with, and maybe sporting a new scar or two. It would have been so much easier if he had stayed asleep.

I tensed, knife in hand, prepared for him to either make a clumsy run at me or unleash the flames of Hell. But he did neither of those things. What he did was worse.

He sat up, tucked his legs under him, and regarded me with solemn eyes. "He warned me you would be coming. He agonized over it—knowing he couldn't be there to protect all of us at once, and understanding what would happen to the ones he left unguarded. I told him it was all right. There are worse things than death—I've seen them now."

Then he smiled, the bastard—a soft, sad little smile that made me want to punch him in the face just to force him to get up off the bed and fight me. "Do what you have to do, Inquisitor. But do it quickly, will you? He will never forgive himself if he thinks I suffered."

Well, wasn't this just a shit-covered capstone to this turd of a day. How was I supposed to slit his throat now, with him looking at me like that, smiling that little smile? I would even have taken an unfair fight over no fight at all. Which might seem a little hypocritical, given that I'd been perfectly willing to kill him while he slept. But if he'd been asleep, he wouldn't have been able to look at me with those cow eyes.

The Enemy could wear many faces, I reminded myself. Some were terrifying. Some were beautiful. Some looked like defenseless humans, trying to stave off their inevitable end by inspiring sympathy. That showed how much this priest knew. He should have known no sympathy existed in an Inquisitor's heart.

"Who said he would protect you?" I asked, even though Michael had told me not to ask any questions. Maybe because Michael had told me not to ask any questions. "Who doesn't want you to suffer?"

The priest shook his head. "If it's information you're here for, I'm afraid you'll be disappointed. I'm prepared to carry these truths to my grave. Some things are too terrible to be spoken aloud—especially to those who can no longer be trusted."

I ground my teeth. He was one to talk. I was here on behalf of the same church he'd sworn to serve. My faith had never wavered. He was the one who had let himself be corrupted.

At least I understood something now. If not the whole picture, then one small part of it. "A servant of the Enemy came to you. He told you these terrible truths." The same visitor Father Andersen had talked about in his journal, if I had to guess.

My instincts had been right—my boss hadn't been the good Father's mysterious visitor. My boss had killed the corrupted Father Andersen, for the same reason I was about to kill the priest sitting in front of me, cow eyes or no. Why he'd done it himself instead of assigning one of us, I didn't know, but if I had to guess, I'd say he was trying to bait out the mysterious visitor.

And it had worked. The visitor had shown up to protect the priest, a little too late, and my boss had gotten the fight he'd been looking for. Only he'd lost.

A sudden cold came over me. I shivered.

The priest laughed softly. "How little you understand."

His eyes darted toward the window—just a quick little glance, but I caught it. My hands tensed around the knife. If this visitor of his had shown up to protect Father Andersen, it wasn't much of a stretch to assume he could show up here at any moment. And this was someone who could take down an angel—a feat I had never seen in all my years serving the Inquisition. And I had seen things that still had me waking in a cold sweat, even years later. If I knew what was good for me, I would stop chatting, finish the job, and get out before I found out firsthand what had killed my boss.

"I'm sorry about this," I found myself saying, even though of course I wasn't—he was a servant of the Enemy, as dangerous and as undeserving of apologies as a poisonous spider. Some days I felt like an assassin—or, in my more bigheaded moments, some kind of holy warrior—but in reality, we were more like Heaven's exterminators. It didn't matter what shape the priest wore; he had stopped being a part of the human race the day he had let the Enemy in.

I looked at the knife, but didn't move. I had to finish the job quick and get out before it was too late—I knew that. But this man knew what had left the center of my moral universe lying dead on the floor of the church, and how, and why. Once I did the job, I would lose that information forever. It wasn't as if Michael was going to tell me anything.

I told myself that was why I didn't want to finish it.

I raised the knife. My faith had never wavered. It would not waver now.

But before I could lower the blade, shadow flickered outside the window. The priest turned his head. A soft sigh escaped him as relief swept across his face.

I froze, torn between doing what I had come here to do, or cutting my losses and making a run for it. Which meant I didn't have the time to do either before the window shattered and a dark shape burst into the room.

The cloaked figure filled the small bedroom. He wasn't big, but he was tall, with a presence bigger than his physical form. Underneath his hood, I caught a glimpse of harsh, angular features, and dark eyes that sent a shiver through me even though he didn't look much more than human. Maybe especially because of that. I liked to know what I was facing.

"What are you?" I asked.

That drew a weary laugh from him. "That's a complicated

question these days, sorry to say. But once, I bowed to the same God as you. I soared through Heaven on wings of fire, and let Him wrap me in golden chains. We're not so different, you and me. Your weapons are your wings. Have you seen the chains yet?"

I let out a sharp hiss. One of the Fallen. I had been fighting their children, the hellspawn, for years. But I had never met one of the Fallen themselves. It was rumored that a handful of Inquisitors, over the centuries, had faced one of them and lived. But those were nothing more than rumors.

The smart thing to do would have been to run for the door. Sure, I didn't have a snowball's chance of outrunning one of the Fallen, but it was still more of a chance than I would have if I stood there gaping like an idiot.

But I stayed where I was, knife held high. Consecrated or not, that puny blade wouldn't give the creature in front of me so much as a paper cut. But if I was going to die tonight—and I didn't see any other way this confrontation could go—I would go down facing my enemy, with a weapon in my hand.

My eyes tried to squeeze shut, to escape the sense of roiling terror that crawled through me at the sight of the thing in front of me. I forced them to stay open, and looked the creature dead in the eye.

Huh. It actually wasn't as bad as meeting Michael's gaze. Apparently even the depths of evil couldn't compare to the gut-melting panic of staring down the concentrated divine power of an archangel head-on. Well, at least I had learned something new before I died.

I held the fallen angel's gaze and waited for the blast of hellfire that would end my life. If I was lucky, it would be quick.

"Kill me and be done with it, servant of the Enemy." I was surprised when my voice didn't shake.

"I serve no one, Inquisitor. Not anymore. But I don't see a way around the part where I kill you, I'm afraid." He reached under his cloak. Moonlight glinted off dark metal. I recognized the lines of a pistol. Since when did the Fallen carry human weapons?

"She didn't like what they sent her here to do," the priest said from behind me. "I could see it in her eyes. Show her mercy."

I wanted to protest that I had never thought of questioning my orders, that I had only hesitated because I had been weighing the benefits of torturing some answers out of him first. But knowing my life was on the line, I clamped my lips shut.

The Fallen looked past me to the priest. "Mercy isn't something the Inquisition knows much about. There's a chance she could be made to see reason, but it's a slim one. And if I spare her life, your own will be in danger. I can't protect you forever."

"Show her mercy," the priest repeated.

The Fallen shrugged one shoulder. "As you say." His eyes met mine again. "It's just as well—I don't like my chances against that arsenal you're carrying anyway."

I frowned. "You took down an angel. You can't expect me to believe you see me as a threat."

"That's not something I'll be able to pull off again, sorry to say. A few weeks back, an uncommonly persistent demon tracked me down out of a misguided sense of hero-worship. I let him give me a gift, so long as he promised not to let Lucifer know where I am. He's not too happy with me, see. The gift was a weapon that could poison an angel's blood. One use only. It's gone now, melted into your angel's veins."

He opened his hands to me. They looked like ordinary human hands. He was wearing a set of fingerless leather gloves. The leather was cracked and worn.

"Why is Lucifer after one of his own?" I asked. "And if he is, why would some demon be so eager to give you a gift?"

"You're asking some complicated questions tonight, Inquisitor." Under his cloak, I caught the hint of a crooked smile. "Wish I had time to answer them."

"Here's a simpler one," I said, hard and fierce, like my heart wasn't trying its best to pound its way out of my chest. "Why'd you kill the head of the Inquisition?"

"I thought I could use my unexpected gift to save a few lives," he said, nodding at the priest. "Do the human race a bit of good." He looked at me, and at my weapons. "Looks like I was wrong on that score."

"If by doing the human race some good, you mean leaving it open to the forces of the Enemy, you almost managed it. But Michael is in charge now. You won't be bringing him down anytime soon." She pictured Michael's eyes, the cold fire burning her straight down to her soul, and shivered.

"There's a lot you don't know, Inquisitor. Somehow I don't think you'll take too kindly to my efforts to cure your ignorance, but I'll give it a go, even so." His voice turned deeper and more formal. "The world is no longer as you knew it, Inquisitor. God is dead, at the hands of the Fallen. The Heavenly Throne you serve is empty. Soon the wars for that Throne will begin, and you and yours will have to choose who to serve."

* * *

I wanted to laugh. So that was the terrible truth Father Andersen had alluded to in his journal. That was what this creature had whispered in the ears of this priest and however many others. All this, for such an obvious lie.

"You don't want to believe," said the Fallen. "I understand. You think if what I say is true, it would be the end of everything, the end of hope. I'm guessing you also won't believe me when I say humanity has been *given* hope, at last, for the first time in all your long history."

"If you're going to kill me, do it," I snapped. "But don't insult me by thinking you can weaken my faith."

"The one you were sent here to kill could have told me to do the same to you," the Fallen pointed out. "He chose to spare your life. Out of respect for him, if nothing else, listen to what I have to say."

"I don't know why he chose to spare my life." That was a lie. I knew what he had seen in me. He had seen weakness. "But I'd rather show respect for the angel who gave me my purpose." My hand tightened on the knife. "The one you killed."

"I'm sorry for what I had to do. Too many of my former brothers have died already. But he chose the wrong master. I hope you won't make the same mistake."

"I only have one master, same as him. And that's not going to change." I pulled my shoulders back, baring my chest to him. Daring him to pull that gun and shoot me center mass. The hilt of my knife was slick with sweat.

"I told you I served Him once." The Fallen lowered his eyes. "I told myself I had no choice. The truth is, I was a coward. I feared the flames of Hell, so I stayed silent and obedient as he ordered me to protect the humans who fed his ego the most and sang his praises the loudest, no matter what sins they indulged in the rest of the time. And some of them did terrible things, Inquisitor. The things I've seen... the worst depravities of Hell can't come close to what some of God's most beloved servants are capable of."

Despite the danger I was in, I rolled my eyes. "Don't talk to me about what humans are capable of. I used to be a cop. Believe me, I've seen it. But now I'm an Inquisitor. Last week I fought a demon who broke into the maternity ward to snack on the newborns. The one the week before was worse. You really want to tell me human evil can hold a candle to what your kind can do?"

He blinked those dark eyes slowly, sorrowfully. "Most of the Fallen are corrupted beyond saving now, it's true. When they first fought to liberate the throne, their cause was a righteous one. I learned that after my own Fall. I learned to question a lot of things I used to believe. But there's no goodness left in their hearts anymore, and their offspring are worse. Living in constant pain and despair, with no chance of an end, will do that. I only stayed true to myself because I knew someday I would..." He shook his head, and didn't finish the sentence. "But we're not here for my story. We're here to find out how yours will end."

"With me taking a bullet or five from that pathetic excuse for a gun, it looks like. So why don't you get on with it, and save me having to listen to your voice any longer?" I knew I should be afraid. But all I felt was the same disappointment as the summer I was ten years old, when I was finally old enough to go on the monster Funville roller coaster. I had heard it had three loops and had made my next-door neighbor's older sister barf so hard fried chicken had come out her nose. But when I had finally gotten on, not only did it not have any loops, it traveled at half speed, like one of the baby rides.

I'd thought if one of the Enemy's servants ever took enough of an interest in me to try and sway me to their side, they'd offer me something impossible to turn down. I'd thought it would take every ounce of willpower in me to walk away. Once in a while, late at night, I had rehearsed what I would say. I'd imagined slicing my own blade down my palm to break myself out of the spell they would surely put me under.

And now that the moment was here, this was the best

they had to offer? I was even talking to one of the Fallen, not some piddling hellspawn. But apparently he didn't have anything more compelling on offer than a little speech about human evil and a story about killing Someone who, by definition, couldn't die. Honestly, how did anyone ever fall for the Enemy's tricks? If I'd had any sympathy left for the idiot humans who did things like summon demons into the world for us to clean up, that would have killed it. The rest of the human race had to be even dumber than I'd thought.

And what thanks would I get for keeping humanity safe for so long? A bullet through the heart, because the priest behind me—and if anyone should have known better, it was a priest—had actually bought into this nonsense.

"Did they tell you a story about divine justice?" the Fallen asked softly. "About punishing evildoers and protecting the innocent? Whatever they told you, you bought into it with all your heart—I can tell. You have the light of a true believer in your eyes. You built your life around their lie. But that's all it ever was. Heaven never cared about the difference between the innocent and the guilty, and it certainly never cared about justice."

This guy sure did know how to talk, didn't he? Much more of this, and I would either shoot him or myself, just to spare me having to listen to him any longer.

Come to think of it, maybe I actually had an opportunity here. He was so in love with the sound of his own voice, maybe he wouldn't notice if I went for my gun. A bullet normally wouldn't do anything against one of the Fallen, but he seemed to think I was a threat. Maybe he was right. My hand inched toward my belt.

His hand shot out to grab my wrist. He glanced down at the gun I'd been going for, just long enough to let me know he knew. Then he let me go and kept on talking as if nothing had happened.

"The One who used to sit on the Throne of Heaven only ever wanted one thing," he said. "To feed His oversized ego. The angels who groveled the most prettily got to share in Heaven's luxuries. The rest of us did the dirty work that kept them where they were. It was the same here on Earth: the humans who praised Him the loudest got protection, wealth, fame. The truly deserving struggled in the gutter. You've seen it yourself, haven't you? There's never been any such thing as justice—not here, and not in Heaven. Only people who know how to work the system, profiting off the backs of everyone else. The day that changed was the day divine blood stained the streets of Heaven, and the Eternal Light winked out."

Okay, that one hurt. For a second, I was standing in the middle of the police station again, feeling myself go suddenly weightless like that day on the front porch as a kid, while someone I had considered a friend fastened a pair of handcuffs around my wrists. I was sitting in that courtroom, watching the gavel come down and smash the world I had known into unrecognizable shards.

I hadn't wanted anything to do with the Inquisition at first. I hadn't wanted to risk believing in another system, another authority figure. And besides, they didn't exactly have a shining reputation. It was only when my boss had shown me his wings that I had said yes. Surely an angel could do no wrong, and the ultimate Authority could never let me down.

"You looked me up, didn't you?" I accused. "Probably read my police file before coming here. You know just what buttons to press. Congratulations."

"Haven't you ever had any doubts—"

"No," I said too quickly, thinking about the shudder that had run through me at Michael's touch. That hadn't been doubt. Just a perfectly understandable reaction at being that close to so much divine power, in the middle of a situation I didn't understand. I didn't like being in the dark. And even if, for second, my confusion had edged toward doubt, I would never admit it to one of the Fallen.

The Fallen still had his mouth open. I realized, too late, that I'd leapt in before he was even done talking. I snapped my lips shut. My face flushed.

He gave me a sad, knowing smile. "Haven't you ever had any doubts about any of the people they've sent you after?" he finished.

"No," I repeated, more confidently this time. My work was something I had never questioned. Find the bad guys. Stop the bad guys. It had a clarity of moral purpose that I had only dreamed of in my police days.

And yet. One memory drifted to the front of my mind. There had been a woman once, a couple of years ago. She'd uncovered a rash of embezzlement in her church, a handful of officials appropriating funds for personal use. I only remembered her because I had read the story in the paper about a week before I had gotten the order. I had cheered out loud when I had read it, and then scowled into my coffee, thinking about how I should have gone to the local paper instead of my superiors all those years ago. Maybe the story would have ended the same way, but at least I would have had the satisfaction of doing some damage to their reputations.

I had been so disappointed when my boss had given me her name. The woman hadn't been a kindred spirit after all. She wasn't some plucky innocent, heroically exposing a hotbed of corruption. She was just one more demonic agent, spreading lies and sowing division to try to bring down the church.

But when I had gone to her house, she had fought back with pepper spray, of all things. No hellfire. No black magic.

Just a goofy little canister she had pulled out of her purse. "They sent you, didn't they?" she had asked, her eyes wide with fear—or a masterful imitation of it, anyway. "They sent you to shut me up."

It hadn't meant anything, of course. The pepper spray. The lack of supernatural power. Her show of fear. Demons used human servants all the time, and didn't bother giving all of them a means to defend themselves. And even if her fear had been real... well, there was a reason the Inquisition's reputation had endured so long. It wasn't only because of the lies the Enemy had spread about us. Hell itself feared us, and for good reason.

Still, though. I had thought about it for a long time afterward. I had wanted so badly to believe in her. To think there was someone else out there fighting the good fight in the mundane world like I used to do, and doing a better job of it than I had. And she had let me down. That was probably why it took me so long to get her out of my head.

Probably.

His eyes drilled into mine. He didn't say anything, but I had the uncomfortable feeling it was because he didn't need to. He could already read my thoughts all over my face.

"I've never doubted the rightness of my purpose," I said, refusing to look away. "And I won't start because of the likes of you."

"517 Garland Street," he said. "Room 312. Be there tomorrow, at seven in the evening. Listen carefully to what you hear there, and don't let yourself be seen. After that, you can decide the truth for yourself."

I didn't move. "That's it? You're letting me go?" I had thought the Fallen were smarter than that. What was to stop me from coming back and finishing the job as soon as he left?

"If you come back here, the man you came here to find will be gone," he said, as if he had read my mind. "And I'll know you've broken the terms of our agreement."

"Now hang on. There hasn't been any agreement. The Inquisition doesn't bargain with—"

He spoke over me. "I'll make it look like you killed the priest. Things will go easier for you with your superiors that way—but only for a little while. After that, you'll need to make your own plans."

"I have a plan. Find out what you're up to, and stop it."

"Tomorrow night," he said. "Seven p.m. For now, leave this place. Rest if you can. You're going to need it."

I hefted the knife in my hand. But I already knew I wouldn't use it. As much as it galled me to let one of the Enemy's creatures leave unharmed, and walk away without finishing the job I'd come here to do, attacking one of the Fallen on my own would be suicide. No matter what he said about his chances against me. The last time the Inquisition had gone up against one of them in person, it had been two dozen Inquisitors against one of the Fallen, and only one person had walked away alive. It hadn't been any of the Inquisitors.

Teeth clenched, cheeks burning with shame, I finally broke his gaze. I shoved the knife back into its sheath, and turned and stalked away.

* * *

517 Garland Street, it turned out, was a local high-end hotel. A group of people representing various business interests from around the state had booked the third-floor conference room for the evening.

My first thought was to use the old trick of masquerading as one of the catering staff and eavesdropping on the meeting from behind the anonymous safety of a uniform. That plan lasted all of five minutes. When I approached my first staff member with an offer to trade places, I found out that not only were these people not taking advantage of the hotel's complementary catering services, they had categorically banned all hotel employees from not just the room but the entire floor for the duration of their meeting. Apparently they had the kind of cash to throw around that made that request start to look reasonable, because according to the person I talked to, the hotel had threatened all the staff with docked wages if they so much as pressed the third-floor button on the elevator while the meeting was going on.

But there was nothing stopping me from booking a room on the fourth floor as an ordinary guest. Or, once I was in there, from drilling a hole in the floor with the tools I had filled my overnight bag with instead of a change of clothes, and snaking a miniature camera down through the ceiling of room 312.

By the time anyone found out about the damage to the room, I would be long gone—or rather, the alias I had rented the room under would be. The hotel would never be able to come after me for the cost of the repairs. I'd already had to eat the cost of the room, though. I winced when I thought about the bill, which covered all kinds of luxuries I wouldn't get the chance to use.

Maybe I'd invoice Declan for expenses. I had a feeling Michael wouldn't look kindly on it if I tried to do the same with him. There was a reason I hadn't called my emergency contact number to report my conversation with the Fallen.

Although I still wasn't quite sure what that reason was. Reporting the contact was the only course of action that made sense. If there really was something going down in that room, it needed a surveillance specialist, or several, not a foot soldier like me. And after having contact with the Fallen, no matter how brief, I needed to be monitored for possible contamination. And yet here I was.

I knew what the Fallen would have said. But he would have been wrong. I wasn't having doubts. I certainly didn't believe that story of his.

I just wanted some answers. That was all.

The trick with the camera was that I had to hold it in place manually. I didn't want to risk doing something like taping it to the floor, only to have it come loose and fall at the wrong moment. I held the attached wire with one hand, With the other, I worked the controls on my laptop. Using my keyboard, I could control the direction it turned, and how loudly the sound came through on my end. Yes, it picked up audio too.

It was a sweet little piece of tech. Courtesy of my old friends at the police department, much as I hated to take anything from them. Declan had given it to me when I asked him if he had anything that would do the job. After I had told him it was related to the angel case, he hadn't even asked for details. Maybe I owed him a Christmas card next year after all.

Movement on the screen caught my attention. Suited men had started filing into the room. I checked my watch. Seven on the dot. I squinted at the screen, and let out my breath when I didn't see any faces I recognized. Not that I'd really thought I was going to find some secret Inquisition conspiracy going on behind my back.

And of course, that was when the last man walked into the room and locked the door behind him. The picture quality wasn't the greatest, but it didn't matter. I knew that face. I knew those eyes.

He was the Archangel Michael.

He sat down at the head of the table. Because I had already recognized him, I wasn't surprised when the human guise fell away, and his flame-streaked wings spread out behind him. What I didn't expect was for everyone else in the room to follow suit. One second, a dozen wealthy businessmen sat at the table. The next, the room was all white wings and eyes that blazed with unearthly fire.

Even through the camera, those eyes were hard to look at. Luckily, none of them spent much time looking up, so mostly I found myself staring at the tops of their heads.

Michael cleared his throat. "You may wonder why we're meeting here on earth, in the squalor that passes for luxury among the humans." His face twisted in disgust. "The situation has worsened since we last met. There are spies everywhere. Until I weed out the disloyal from our ranks, Heaven is no longer safe."

The picture jerked as I almost lost control of the camera. I'd known something bad was going down. I had known it ever since the body in the church. But to hear an archangel saying Heaven itself wasn't safe... well, it got me wondering if maybe poor old Father Andersen hadn't been right in his choice of reading material.

"Gabriel is missing," Michael continued. "Uriel has officially gone rogue. At least two other factions have formed among the lesser angels. Most humans don't yet know the Throne is empty, but we won't be able to keep it from them forever. The Fallen are already spreading rumors."

He paused as the others shifted and muttered uncomfortably, taking in his words.

"The one piece of good news," he said, "is that I have the Inquisition under my control. This will help us maintain order here on Earth, in the face of potential demonic—or angelic—rebellion."

Angelic rebellion. The wire slid along my suddenly-sweaty palm. I was in over my head here. I really should have reported what the Fallen had told me, instead of playing lone cowboy.

On the other hand, if I had reported it, the report would have gone straight to... well, to Michael. The one sitting down there in that room right now. The one who had told me not to ask questions.

The rest of what he had said didn't hit until a few seconds later—but when it did, it hit like a Mack truck. I sagged back onto the carpet, my muscles suddenly as weak and shaky as if I had just come out of an hours-long fight. It was all I could to do keep my hold on the camera.

The humans don't know the Throne is empty.

The Throne is empty.

The words rattled through my suddenly-empty head.

Then it was true? That impossible story only an idiot would have believed—it was true?

God was dead. The Enemy had won.

I forced myself back up to sitting as Michael started talking again. "As of now, you are the only ones I know I can trust. I need to be assured I will keep your loyalty. The other factions will make you tempting offers. Maybe some of them already have." He paused, and held the gaze of an angel sitting close to the opposite end of the table. "Maybe some of you have accepted."

He stalked across the room. A ripple of fear rolled through the other angels at the table.

He drew his fist back and drove it through the angel's heart.

The angel screamed as fire spread outward from the wound to consume him. It took him a long time to burn—and through it all, the room was silent except for his screams. Then even those died away. Another moment later, and there was nothing left of him but a few blackened feathers. Smoke drifted up through the small hole I'd drilled. I held my breath to keep from coughing.

"I trust that serves as a sufficient demonstration of what

will happen if you betray me," said Michael, as he calmly strode across the room to pick up the weapon. "But it's an easy enough fate to avoid. All you have to do is support me when I make my bid for the Throne. If you stand by my side, you may even have the chance for a more prestigious position." He gestured to the charred feathers on the floor. "There will undoubtedly be openings."

He smiled. No one else did.

"Some of you are afraid," he said. "You have doubts. You wonder what shape the new order will take, and maybe even whether someone else might be able to offer you more than I can." His voice took on the soothing cadences of a preacher. "You have nothing to worry about. After I take the Throne, nothing needs to change. We'll cast all those who stood against us into Hell—that's what it's there for. And then? Then we'll lie back and listen to the humans' pretty songs, and grant them a miracle or two if they kiss our feet. The only difference is that now they'll be singing to *us*."

His smile widened into a wolfish grin. "Once I'm sitting on the Throne, I'll have the power to force humans and angels alike to fall to their knees before my loyal soldiers—all of you, if you stick with me. But to reach that point, I'll need your help. Listen closely—this is my plan."

He started talking about Uriel, and other angels with longer names, and heavenly politics I didn't have the context to understand. But I didn't think that was why I couldn't think straight all of a sudden.

A small, desperate part of my mind screamed out that this was a trick. An illusion. It had to be. The Fallen I had met was doing this somehow, to lure me to his side.

But I knew better. I had known better the second Michael had touched me.

It was true. Heaven was every bit as corrupt as here on earth. Not God Himself—whatever the Fallen had said, I wouldn't, couldn't, believe that. But God wasn't there anymore.

How was it the Fallen had put it? The Eternal Light had winked out. All that was left was darkness. Heaven was watching—and the angels watching over us were monsters.

A strange new sound cut through Michael's words. It sounded like a human, wailing and carrying on like the world was ending. It wasn't until I pulled the camera up and shut off the laptop that I realized the sound was coming from me.

* * *

I didn't cry for long. I'd never been much of a crier. When I was eleven years old, I broke my arm so badly I could see a splinter of white bone jutting out from my skin. I didn't even cry then. I sat silently in that hard plastic emergency-room chair, staring down at my own bone and biting my lip.

It's not natural, my mother used to tell me. *You could try to feel* something. She didn't understand that it wasn't as if I didn't feel anything. It was just that I didn't see any point in going leaky-eyed over it. Tears didn't come naturally to me; they were something I had to work for, and they never seemed worth the trouble.

I'd only *really* cried, the blotchy-faced snotty-nosed headachey kind of cry, a handful of times in my life. Each time, I had gotten that weightless feeling, like I was hovering above my body wondering who that pathetic wreck on the floor was. Tonight was the fourth time, maybe the fifth. My guilty verdict had been the third.

So what did I do after the tears stopped? Well, first I took a soak in my hotel room's oversized hot tub. If the world was going to hell anyway, why not take a few minutes to enjoy the small things?

The fancy soap turned out to be disappointing. It smelled like vanilla and peaches. I preferred bracing, woodsy scents. But I turned the water up hot enough to hurt, and that blanked out everything else for a while.

I left after that. I figured I might as well go back to my apartment for what I was planning next. Why make things more difficult for the hotel staff? The hole I had left in their floor would be bad enough.

The whole way back, I was afraid I'd float all the way out of my body, and the empty shell left in the driver's seat would cause an accident while I was off somewhere in the ether. I couldn't feel the seat under me, or the steering wheel in my hands. I couldn't feel gravity holding me down.

I was still numb and weightless when I unlocked my apartment door. The apartment was cold and dark. I didn't even have a dog to greet me, and for the first time, I thought about how depressing that was. I had never needed anything or anyone except my holy purpose, only now that was gone, and I had nothing.

Oh well—it was for the best anyway. I would have had to figure out what to do with a dog, if I had one. Drop it at a neighbor's house or something. Pawn it off on Declan.

I sat down on my bed with its hospital corners. Why had I even kept up that habit anyway? I'd been doing it since I was ten. A little dose of order every morning, like an incantation to hold off the chaos of the world. I fought monsters for a living; I should have known better than anyone that there was more chaos out there than a neatly-made bed could hold at bay.

I took out one of my pistols. Each bullet had been doused in holy water, which meant I really should be reserving the weapon for demons, so as not to waste the ammo. Well, if anyone objected, they could send a formal letter of complaint to wherever I ended up.

"If I still have a purpose here, then stop me," I said aloud.

I knew nothing would happen, of course. That didn't stop me from glancing toward the window, as if I thought I might see an angel standing there, ready to burst through the glass and save my life. Yeah, I know, ridiculous. Remember what I said about my bigheaded moments? This was one of them.

There was no angel at the window. No booming voice from Heaven. I waited another moment, just in case. All I heard was the faint skritching of mice in the walls.

Well, there was no sense in sitting here letting the anticipation get to me. I held my breath, stuck the barrel in my mouth, and pulled the trigger.

The gun clicked. Nothing else happened. It took me a few seconds to breathe again, and a few more to realize the gun had jammed.

I didn't know whether to laugh or cry. In the end, I didn't do either. I also didn't reach for the second pistol, even though it was right there. I just sat there on the bed, running my hand back and forth along the taut top sheet over and over, like I was stuck in a loop.

It would have been easier if I hadn't felt so relieved at the fact that I was still breathing.

My phone pinged, making me jump. Probably Declan looking for an update, ignoring what I had said about how he should pretend he'd never gotten involved in any of this. Either that, or someone trying to sell me penis enlargement pills. Either way, I could safely ignore it. But I found myself reaching for my phone anyway.

It was an email. The name in the sender field was *A. Friend.* Against my better judgment, I opened it. All it said was, *Choose your allies carefully. I hope you consider me one of them.* Under that, there was a list of names. Even before I plugged the names one by one into a search engine, I knew what I would find. Priests, all of them. The other targets

Michael had handed out?

A friend. An ally. I let out a single harsh bark of a laugh. More like the Enemy, or at least one of his creatures. I knew who had sent this.

My finger hovered over the delete button.

But I didn't look at the button. I looked at the names. I wondered why exactly Michael wanted these priests dead. Because they knew the truth? Because they didn't want to kiss his feet? An Inquisitor knelt to no one but God. Shouldn't the same be true for a priest? I wondered if Michael would start killing my fellow Inquisitors if they refused to kneel.

I wouldn't be around to find out, of course. I lowered my free hand to the other pistol.

If I did what I was planning, the only difference between me and the priests on that list was that I'd be doing Michael's job for him.

With a huff, I dropped the phone to the bed without deleting the email.

Maybe this was how it started. Giving in to temptation. Letting corruption in. My stomach dropped out from under me, like I was sitting at the top of a roller coaster, waiting for the dizzy fall.

But I could feel it. Not just my stomach, but the ache in my temples, and the scratchy fabric of the cheap sheet under me. I was back in my body again.

I grabbed the phone and typed out a reply. *I do this my way. I'll protect them for now. But at the first sign of demonic corruption, they die.*

I almost sent it, but stopped. I added one last line. *Also, I don't work for you or your master.*

The answer came almost immediately. *I have no master. But understood.*

That was it. I supposed the rest was up to me.

I shoved the phone into my pocket, replaced the magazine in the bum pistol, and headed for the door. It was going to be a long night.

DEVIL'S CROSSROADS

The chess tables weren't busy this time of year. Most of the humans in the city were at home huddling in front of their heaters, packing on the sweater after sweater until they looked like the snowmen that watched us with their judgmental button eyes from across the park. The rest were hurrying down the sidewalk as fast as possible, hands jammed in their pockets, heads ducked against the wind. But the cold didn't bother me. Half the reason I'd come up to Earth was to get away from the heat. As for the angel across from me... well, for him, it was either stay here or go home.

"Checkmate." I tipped his king over and flashed him a quick grin. "That's three in a row. Maybe if you showed up for our games a bit more consistently, you'd get enough practice to beat me once in a while. Where were you last week?"

"Not all of us are as lax about our duties as you are." That stick-up-his-ass voice didn't belong on the body he was currently wearing. He liked to dress up as a goth kid these days. Went by the name of Onyx. With that droopy hair and those depressing black clothes, he looked like he had fallen into a vat of self-indulgent misery and decided to roll around awhile. Which suited him, I supposed. Besides, I liked it a whole lot better than the tech-bro phase this had replaced.

He still stank of angel, though, whatever he was wearing. No amount of—I sniffed, and wrinkled my nose—cedar-and-patchouli cologne could cover that up.

"Duties?" I raised an eyebrow. "Does your boss even know where you are right now? For that matter, has your boss known what you've been up to for the past five hundred years?"

Onyx—he always insisted I use his ridiculous human names, probably in case one of the big guy's spies was listening—started setting up the chessboard again. He made me take black, of course. He always made me take black. "Not all duties are imposed from without," he said without looking up from his work.

So pretentious. Sometimes I didn't know why I put up with him. But every time I tried spending time with my own people—self-important pricks, the lot of them—I remembered all over again. Onyx over there was in the same boat as me, at least when it came to how little we liked our supposed allies. I supposed that meant we were stuck with each other.

If only he would get the memo and stop skipping half our weekly chess games. If he would take his head out of his own ass for five seconds and realize these self-imposed duties of his didn't exist, he might see that I was the only friend he had, and that maybe he had better not take that friendship for granted.

"In that case, maybe you should quit slacking off and get

to work," I said irritably. "What's on the agenda for today? Steal money from the church collection plate and give it to the orphanage? Tsk, tsk. What *would* Daddy say?"

Onyx didn't answer. He silently slid a pawn across the board.

That was all right with me. Onyx had two love languages, affectionate silence and prickly silence, and it was damned hard to tell the difference between the two. *Angels.* Sometimes I thought half the reason I Fell was so I wouldn't have to hang around that lot anymore. And yet here I was, staying out in the winter chill to wipe the floor with one of them for the fourth time today. He could have at least had the decency to make it a challenge for me.

I moved my pawn. "It's never too late to choose a new path, you know. You might find Hell a nice change of pace. Who knows, it might even loosen you up a bit. Full of sex, drugs, and rock 'n' roll, or so I'm told. I wouldn't know—I haven't set foot in the place since before rock 'n' roll existed."

"I'll pass on that generous and not at all self-serving offer," said Onyx expressionlessly, as he made a move that would win me the game in five turns. "The power struggles of the Fallen don't interest me."

"Hey, same here. Why do you think I'm here freezing my ass off, preparing to hand yours to you yet again?"

Before Onyx could make another losing move, his phone buzzed. I leaned back with a sigh and settled in for a staring contest with the snowmen as he pulled it from his pocket. "Yes, what is it? I told you I wasn't to be disturbed this afternoon."

Aww, wasn't that sweet—he had blocked out time in his busy schedule of lies, theft, and blasphemy for me. I guess even he couldn't steal from his boss and give to the starving orphans every hour of the day.

I made a blah-blah-blah motion with my hand as I let his

words slide past me. I knew I should probably be listening in. Always a good idea to know what the other side was up to. But I had lost all interest in Heaven's drama a couple thousand years ago. I drummed my fingers on the table, and wondered if one of those snowmen might make a better opponent. It wasn't like Onyx was much more talkative than an inanimate lump of snow. Or much better at chess, either.

When Onyx hung up, his mouth was a grim line. Without a word, he started packing the chess pieces away.

I frowned. "What, not even a goodbye? Guess I'll have to challenge one of those snowmen to a game after all. They might be more gracious losers."

Onyx didn't answer. I took a closer look at his face. Instantly, I wished I hadn't made the crack. This was more than his usual trouble-at-the-hypothetical-orphanage look. Something was really wrong. The last time I had seen that look on his face, it turned out the Archangel Michael had picked up his trail, and he had spent the previous week on the run with no sleep.

"What is it? Your boss finally realize you were missing?" I tried my best to walk the line between "supportive friend" and "casually unconcerned," but I was pretty sure I just came across sounding like an asshole.

He paused halfway through tucking the last pawn away. I saw him think about walking away without giving me an answer. Then he set the pawn down and met my eyes.

I shivered. I couldn't remember the last time I had met an angel's gaze straight-on. Terrifying, was what it was. All that suppressed rage, packed into that itty-bitty human form. You could say one thing for the Fallen—we at least knew how to let our anger out.

"God is dead," Onyx said flatly.

I stared at him, waiting for the punch line. It didn't come.

"You're talking about your boss," I said, just to be sure.

"The man upstairs. The big kahuna."

"One of the Fallen is responsible, or that's what I heard. It sounds like no one knows much of anything just yet. Only that the Heavenly Light has been extinguished, and the Divine Throne stands empty." He flicked the pawn over with a finger.

I spent a good few seconds just trying to figure out how such a thing was possible. If God could be killed, surely one of us would have done it long before now. But then, it wasn't like Heaven's armies had given us much of a chance. The whole war had been pretty one-sided. I blamed it on all the lazy-ass angels who could have joined us but chose to sit on the sidelines, waiting to see who the victor would be before they decided who to support.

I spared another couple of seconds wondering who had succeeded where the rest of us had failed, and how. Then I remembered I didn't care.

But this news was going to have a major impact back home, whether it was true or not. I had a good long think about the prospect of every demon in Hell simultaneously setting their own schemes into motion to take full advantage of the chaos they would all see coming.

I took a deep breath of frigid winter air, and tried not to choke on angel-stink.

"Well," I said mildly, "fuck."

* * *

When I got home, Beelzebub was in my apartment. He had plunked his sweaty, sulfur-smelling ass down on my expensive leather couch, and was currently flipping through one of my magazines. When I slammed the door behind me, he stood up, snapped to attention, and fired off a salute.

I met his salute with a roll of my eyes. "Isn't this a nice

surprise," I said, not bothering to conceal my sarcasm.

"The forces of Hell await your orders," he said, with all the personality of one of those talking dolls little girls get for Christmas. No, never mind—the average talking doll was a far better conversationalist than Beelzebub.

"And?" I took the spot that he had vacated, put my feet up on the coffee table, and picked up the magazine he had abandoned. *Culinary Life Monthly.* I really had to get around to making those key lime bars on the cover one of these days.

He blinked down at me. I could see the rusty gears turning in his head as he tried to figure out whether it was more of a breach of etiquette to sit down in the presence of his supreme commander, or to stay standing while said commander was lounging on the couch. I could have stood back up and made things easier on him. I didn't.

I turned the page. *You Voted! Readers' Fifty Favorite Christmas Cookie Recipes.* I wondered which I should try first. I was something of a Grinch when it came to Christmas, for obvious reasons, but I would never turn down an opportunity for cookies.

After several visibly painful seconds of frozen confusion, Beelzebub chose to stay standing. "When do we attack? Have you formulated a battle plan?"

I shrugged and turned another page. "Isn't it your job to figure that stuff out? Why else have I been paying you to keep my seat warm all these centuries?"

This time, Beelzebub's blink had a decidedly startled tone. "Lord Lucifer?"

I clenched my jaw. I hated titles. Reminded me too much of home, where everyone was General this and Archangel that, the better to know whose divine ass to kiss. "You heard me. If you want to attack so badly, figure it out. Stamp my name on it, if you insist."

"Lord Lucifer, that... that would not be proper."

"And if there's one thing we care about in Hell, it's being proper." I tossed the magazine aside. Beelzebub clearly wasn't going to let me concentrate on Christmas cookies this afternoon. "You want orders? Fine. Go back home and do nothing. Plant your ass back down on my throne, think up some creative punishments for the lesser hellspawn when they get too uppity, and pretend like nothing has changed. Because it hasn't. Not for us." I could hope, couldn't I? If Hell got itself drawn into a war, I would never squeeze any baking in.

"Lord Lucifer, you… you *have* heard the news?"

"Stop *calling* me that." I was starting to understand why my angelic friend insisted I use his human name. Maybe his title weighed as heavily on him as mine did on me. "Yes. I heard. And I've already told you what I plan to do about it—exactly nothing. What's the point of leaving Heaven if we still have to pay attention to every little thing that happens there?"

A little tension crept into my voice. I forced my jaw to unclench. "This doesn't concern us," I said, to myself as much as to Beelzebub. "Not if we don't want it to."

"I would remind my lord that we did not leave Heaven by choice," said Beelzebub stiffly—although really, that was redundant when it came to Beelzebub. If there was anyone who had more of a stick up his ass than my angelic friend, it was my second-in-command. "We were forced out, when our revolution failed. Now the throne stands empty. This is our chance to make another attempt. We may not get another."

"You're getting a little loud there, Bub." I picked the magazine back up and leafed through it again. But my heart wasn't in it anymore. Neither was my stomach. Looking at all those cookies only made me queasy. I flipped past a picture of cherry frosting, and all I could see was blood and fire.

I'd had my fill of war in our first attempted coup. And then I'd gotten stuck with a throne, on top of everything else. I had no desire to find out what I'd get stuck with if we made another go of it. The pointy end of Michael's sword, maybe.

I watched Beelzebub curiously over the top of the magazine, waiting to see whether he would voice an objection to the nickname I knew he hated. Instead, he dropped his gaze to his shiny shoes. "I apologize, Lord Lucifer. I forget myself."

Disappointing. Maybe one of these days he would grow a backbone. "Yes. You do. Now run along home, will you? You stink of hell. The last time one of you came around, I got a written complaint from my landlord."

Beelzebub glanced toward the door, but stayed where he was. I raised my eyebrows. Beelzebub not obeying a direct order? Huh. Maybe things were worse than I thought.

My stomach lurched. I set the magazine down.

"The choice of whether to mount an attack is, of course, yours," said Beelzebub. "But there are still matters to attend to back home. No small number of your subjects will take this as open season on the humans. If you wish to discourage the sort of behavior Heaven's forces formerly kept in check, you will need to act swiftly and decisively, and make a strong example of any wrongdoers. For this, I cannot act in your stead. They will need to see your face, and hear your voice."

That was one of the things I'd been trying not to think about. Every demon had their own way of dealing with the torments of Hell. The fire that always burned under the skin, whether we were down in the pit or walking the human world. The loneliness and despair that dogged us like twin gray shadows. All part of the curse the big boss had placed on the Fallen—the curse we had transmitted to our children, the hellspawn. And in this new world, some of those coping mechanisms could be rather... apocalyptic.

Some demons, mainly the original Fallen, were preoccupied with returning to Heaven and finishing what they had started. Even now, thousands of years later, they couldn't let it go. Others threw themselves into playing Hell's power games. They earned respect through extravagant shows of strength, or proved themselves in subtler ways by luring human souls to Hell. These were the ones who made pilgrimages to my throne to prostate themselves at my feet and show me their necklace of skulls or tally of corrupted souls. As if I cared one whit for their amusements. All those demons falling over each other to kiss my feet... they were half the reason I had left Hell and plunked Beelzebub down on the throne in my place.

And then there was me.

I felt the pain of the flames as much as any of them. And the loneliness, and the despair. Those two were good friends of mine by now. I didn't see any point in going through all the trouble of trying to return home just to be rid of them, or distracting myself with games of power. I just wanted to play a satisfying game of chess against a worthy opponent, and then come back home to experiment with a new recipe or two. Was that too much to ask?

But then there were the other demons, the ones Beelzebub was worried about. They didn't want to stop the pain by returning back home, or distract themselves by winning their imaginary competitions. They embraced it all as part of their nature. They didn't just feel the pain and the despair; they *were* pain and despair. They reveled in it, gloried in it, searched for new and clever ways to inflict it on others. They were the ones most likely to cause noisy chaos up here on Earth and bring the vengeance of Heaven down on the rest of us. And they were the ones who would bring Hell to Earth now that the cat was away, if no one stepped in to stop them.

In theory, stopping them was my job. The rest of the

Fallen had crowned me as their leader, despite my protests. And it wasn't like I was looking forward to my subjects turning Earth into their personal playground. I liked my peace and quiet. Both of which I would get precious little of if my demons started marching down the streets, pillaging and burning. If I had wanted to watch things burn, I could have stayed home.

But I had walked away for a reason. That reason being, I was sick and tired of herding demons. It was worse than herding cats—at least the cats didn't talk back. I had never asked for the job, and as far as I was concerned, I had more than earned my retirement.

And I didn't see why that should have to change just because the man upstairs had seen fit to go and die on us.

So I shook my head, and ignored the sensation of a school of fish swimming figure-eights in my stomach. "Not my problem. You want to try and stop them, go right ahead. I'll even give you a pay raise. As long as you walk out that door in the next thirty seconds. Starting... now." I tapped my wrist, where a watch would have been if I had bothered to wear one.

Beelzebub still didn't move. Well, he could kiss that raise goodbye. I frowned and sat up straight. "Well? What are you waiting for?" As much as I hated to do it, I put a bit of steel into my voice this time, and tried to sound like the commander he wanted me to be.

"Lord Lucifer." Beelzebub looked green. If it was possible, his voice sounded a shade more formal than it had a second ago. "Your realm and your people require your personal attention. You have neglected both for far too long."

I blinked. Well then. Had my second-in-command found himself a backbone after all? I smiled like a proud papa. "Good for you, Bub."

He shot a sharp, confused glance down at me. When I

didn't say anything else, he went back to standing at attention. "If you will not return home to Hell and take command, then you…" He swallowed and soldiered on. "Then you are unfit to lead. I have no choice but to make a formal challenge for the throne of Hell."

"Sure, go ahead. It's yours." I leaned back and laced my hands together behind my head. The fish in my stomach stopped their frantic swimming. Why hadn't I ever thought of that? If I had realized it was that easy to rid myself of the throne, I would have pushed Beelzebub to make a challenge a long time ago.

"Lord Lucifer? Did you not hear what I said?"

"I heard you. You're king of the hill now. Congratulations. I'll send you down a batch of cookies for your coronation. Or swearing-in, or however you want to do it. Which do you prefer, chocolate chip or gingerbread?" I shook my head. "Never mind. Silly question. Everyone likes chocolate chip best."

The green tinge didn't leave Beelzebub's face. If anything, it was worse now. "We must have a formal trial by combat."

Without getting up, I made a few halfhearted air punches. "There. We fought. I lost. All hail the champion. Now hurry on back home, will you, and make it official."

"This… this is not how things are done."

Hell preserve me from subordinates with more loyalty than brains. "Who says? In all the history of Hell, it's only ever had one supreme dictator. Me. So remind me, who precisely made the rules that govern the transfer of power? Was it me? Because if it was, chalk that one up to a drunken mistake."

Beelzebub still didn't look convinced. Worse, he wasn't leaving.

I heaved a sigh they could probably hear all the way back home. "Do you want me to make a formal decree of it? Here you go. I, Lucifer, hereby declare that Beel—"

The opening bars to "Highway to Hell" blasted through the apartment, interrupting me. I scowled and looked around. Beelzebub, a sheepish look on his face, reached for his cell phone.

"Don't answer that," I snapped, but he already had. He wasn't even doing a good job of disguising his relief at the interruption.

As he turned away and murmured into the phone in a low voice, I looked down at my biceps and gave them an experimental flex. I sighed. I had really let myself go lately. Too many batches of cookies, not enough people to share them with. I blamed Onyx. I would happily have given him all he could eat, but no, every time I invited him over for a meal he had widows and orphans to save.

It would be his fault, then, if Beelzebub insisted on this trial by combat and I lost. Not that I would shed too many tears about losing my throne, but I was certain my second-in-command had a fight to the death in mind. Getting to walk away from the throne would be small consolation in that case. It would be hard to enjoy a chocolate chip cookie warm from the oven after I had ceased to exist.

Of course I always had my angelic powers to draw on. At least in theory. The Fall might have corrupted the fragment of divine power I had stolen from Heaven, but it had done nothing to dim its strength. No, that had come later. In the revolution, I had set the battlefield aflame, fueled by my belief in my righteous cause. Now, though... what did I believe in? Being left alone? That wasn't enough to light a match with. I hadn't been able to create so much as a spark in centuries.

Beelzebub hung up the phone and turned back to me. "I apologize, Lord Lucifer. We will continue this discussion later. I have just received word of the location of the

Archangel Uriel. If our forces move quickly, we have the opportunity to remove him from play."

The fish started up their swimming again.

"Apparently he reached out to one of the lesser Fallen, and offered to join together to protect Earth from the worst elements of Heaven and Hell." Beelzebub laughed. "The Fallen, of course, reached out to me. They all know better than to trust the word of an angel."

"What if he meant it?" I found myself asking. "Not five minutes ago, you were looking for a way to keep Hell under control."

Beelzebub's poker face shattered. He looked like a debutante who had stumbled into a naked mud-wrestling competition. "By betraying our own people to the forces of Heaven, Lord Lucifer?"

"Fine, then. Tell Uriel no, and let's get on with that trial by combat. I'll even let you choose the weapons." With any luck, that would be a nice distraction for him. My flabby muscles would simply have to rise to the challenge.

"The Fallen in question has already set up a meeting with him," said Beelzebub. "Apparently he has been living in an apartment only a few streets away from here. He has probably been spying on you for quite some time. I assume you would prefer that I handle this, instead of personally involving yourself."

I rose from the couch. The fish in my stomach were doing the Macarena. "Actually, I think I'll take care of this one."

"Lord Lucifer." That didn't sound like the tone of someone who was ready to obediently accept my orders. Also, the green was back in his face again. "I... am afraid I must decline your assistance. Your earlier suggestion has left me troubled. I am afraid you would not act in the best interests of Hell."

Why had he even bothered to ask me whether I wanted him to handle this, if he wasn't going to take no for an answer? "I suggested hearing the guy out. That's all."

"You entertained the possibility of an alliance with the enemy. I apologize for speaking out of turn, Lord Lucifer, but your extended stay on Earth has clearly had an effect on your mind. And although I am truly sorry, I must do what is in the best interests of our people. I will handle the archangel. Then we will have our challenge."

"Why wait? Let's do this. You and me, right now." I reached for the power that had once set Heaven ablaze. But of course nothing happened. Not even a wisp of smoke.

"I am afraid this meeting will not wait. As I said, we will continue this later." Beelzebub started to bow, caught himself halfway through, and froze with his spine at an unnatural angle. It took him a couple of seconds to straighten. I was still trying to wake up my magic when he all but fled for the door. Spineless coward.

I stared at the door he had disappeared through as the fish started into the Electric Slide. "Saint Peter's hairy ballsack," I muttered. "I'm going to have to do something about this, aren't I?"

* * *

I had never set foot in Onyx's apartment before, but if I had ever cared enough to imagine it, this was what I would have pictured. A single room, walls painted a spartan gray. A barracks-style cot in one corner, a sad olive-green 1970s-style refrigerator in the other. No magazines, of course. I doubted his oh-so-busy schedule left him much time for reading.

Every detail was exactly what I had expected. Right down to the two Fallen wearing human guises, pinning Onyx down in the center of the floor, as Beelzebub stood over them with arms crossed and his best stern second-in-command face on.

The other two had left their poker faces at home. They stared hungrily at Onyx with sadistic grins. One of them was busy carving unholy signals into his pale flesh. The other had pulled on the corrupted divine fire within to ignite a small flame between two fingertips—a flame he was slowly lowering toward Onyx's right eye. With his other hand, he held the eye open so Onyx couldn't squeeze it shut.

They were all so absorbed in their work that none of them noticed the door quietly click shut behind me. Not even Beelzebub, who really should have been standing guard, since it looked like he was doing fuck-all else. Maybe he just liked to watch.

"What we want from you is simple, angel," said the one holding the flame. His face looked vaguely familiar—I had probably known his name back in my revolutionary days. I was sure I could have called it to mind if I spent the time to think about it, but I didn't see why I should bother.

"Change into your angelic form," he continued. "Let us pluck those precious feathers from your wings. If you give us that gift, we'll grant you a clean death. Beg prettily enough, and we'll even wait to strip your wings until after you're dead." The flame crept a little closer. "But if you insist on making things difficult..."

"I've heard if you damage an angel's human shell enough, they have no choice but to change form," said the Fallen wielding the knife, with a nasty little giggle. "It's a reflex. Like when you hit a human's knee in the right place, and their leg kicks out. Or that's what I've heard." With no more warning than that, he brought the knife down to Onyx's knee and angled it in just under the kneecap.

Onyx shrieked and bucked. Beelzebub hastily bent down to hold his shoulders before he could wrench free. So my second-in-command still remembered how to make himself useful after all.

Served Onyx right, for choosing such a flimsy human body this time around. He was so thin and breakable—what had he really expected? If he was going to insist on depriving himself of his best advantage with that senseless vow of his, he could have at least compensated a bit in the physical-strength department. Unlike me, he could choose the details of his human form—one of the perks of uncorrupted angelic power. And what had he chosen? Weakness.

Not that it was really a surprise. He could have killed them off the second they had walked in the door, if he had chosen. He had the power of an archangel at his command. A snap of his fingers, and those two lackeys would have dissolved in white light. Beelzebub would have taken a bit more effort, but that was why archangels kept those big honking swords around, wasn't it?

But he had done nothing. Three demons had entered his inner sanctum, and he had let them. They had held him down and tortured him, and he had lain there and taken it. All because he had sympathized with our cause, back in the day. Not enough to join us, of course, oh no. Just enough to feel guilty afterward about the side he had chosen, and take a vow to never use his angelic power against the forces of Hell.

His vow did nothing to change what had happened to us. But it made him feel better about himself, and that was what mattered, wasn't it?

Self-righteous bastard. A coward in vigilante clothing, working against the man upstairs in secret and pretending that was enough. We could have gone that route, me and every one of my soldiers. We could have taken the easy way. Instead we had gambled it all, and we had lost.

And then the centuries and millennia of torture had twisted the minds of every one of my soldiers, until they couldn't even remember the cause we had fought for. Until all they cared about was power and scheming and sadistic, mindless cruelty.

Maybe the pain had changed me, too. Because when was the last time I had cared about anything? I wasn't even sure I cared enough to be here right now. Maybe, I thought, I should slip right back out the door and be done with it. Onyx—no, might as well call him Uriel, why bother keeping up the pretense anymore?—had brought this on himself with that pointless vow. With the cowardice that had let him keep his place in Heaven while we burned.

But if I did that, who would I trounce at chess every week? I needed some way to feed my ego, and Uriel and his piss-poor chess game fit the bill nicely. He would be hard to replace, if my subjects killed him.

I took a step forward and cleared my throat. "Tsk, tsk. Have you forgotten everything I taught you? Senses sharp, at least one person standing guard at all times, and *never* let someone sneak up behind you." With that, I closed the distance and deftly plucked the knife from the hands of the Fallen.

Their heads all jerked up at once—a few seconds too late, which might as well have been a lifetime as far as they were concerned, because I had already disarmed one of them. I could have killed them all by now if I had been at my full strength. With talent like this on our side, no wonder we had lost the war.

The two lesser Fallen gawked up at me like I had caught them with their hands in the cookie jar. Beelzebub, though, met my gaze with a steady stare. "I told you I would handle this, Lord Lucifer."

"And I told *you* to leave it to me, but it looks like you didn't listen, doesn't it? So much for your famed obedience." I looked away, dismissing him, and instead met the eyes of the two terrified Fallen in turn. "You're here against my direct orders. But I'm guessing Bubby there didn't tell you that part, so I'll let you off the hook for now. Go back to Hell. Don't let me see you pulling something like this again. For that matter, don't let me see you. Ever."

For a few seconds, they couldn't figure out what to do, seeing as it was physically impossible to run for the exit while simultaneously bowing and scraping at my feet. They settled for scurrying toward the door with their shoulders hunched, nodding frantically to me over their shoulders.

Uriel was still lying on the floor, even though they weren't holding him down anymore. He was in worse shape than I thought. Maybe it hadn't been just his vow keeping him where he was. There was blood pooling under him, a lot of blood, more than could be explained by the decorations the Fallen had carved into his skin. I swallowed and looked away.

"Stay where you are," Beelzebub snapped at the fleeing Fallen. They froze, their faces full of terrified confusion as they looked from me to Beelzebub and back again.

A wave of pure loathing swept through me. This was what had become of my proud army? There was a time when my soldiers would have bowed to no one.

I kept my voice calm, almost pleasant, as I addressed Beelzebub. "You wanted me to start giving orders again. Well, here I am. Leave this place, and never come back."

"You know what this one is, do you not?" Beelzebub nudged Uriel with his toe, as if the archangel was a bit of roadkill he had stumbled across. Uriel let out a low moan and tried to curl in on himself. He couldn't move even that much.

"Did I ask for excuses? No. I asked for obedience. *Leave.*"

"With the feathers from his wings, we would have the power to storm the gates of Heaven while their defenses are at their weakest," said Beelzebub. "Once, you would not have hesitated."

"Once, my army stood for something besides senseless torture." I tried to force my eyes away from Uriel. But they kept going right back to him, like the archangel's bleeding body was exerting some kind of magnetic pull.

And yet, I knew Beelzebub was right. Time was, I would have ordered this myself. An angel feather was the only thing that could free a demon from the curse of Hell and let them enter Heaven. A little joke on the big guy's part, that, seeing as all our wings got burned to cinders when we fell.

He didn't really think that one through, though. He failed to consider what it would mean for his people if they were carrying the one thing we wanted above all else on their backs.

Or maybe he just didn't give two shits about whether he put his angels in danger, as long as he could have his little laugh at our expense.

But times changed. And we all changed with them, like it or not. Not always for the worse, either. I missed the passionate revolutionary I had once been, but I wasn't so sure I could say the same for the ruthless newly-Fallen angel who would have ordered Uriel tortured and his wings plucked to bare bone. However much of a spineless coward the archangel was.

Besides, all that revolution stuff had been too much damned work. No time for the simple things in life. Like a soft, melty chocolate chip cookie. Or a good chess game. Even a horribly one-sided chess game.

"This is your final warning. Obey your lord and commander, or face the consequences." I barely recognized the voice that rolled through the room like a low crack of thunder. My voice had sounded like that once, but that had been a long time ago. Even Uriel's eyes widened as he stared up at me.

The two lesser Fallen scurried out the door, and probably

straight back to Hell. I was glad they had left before they pissed their pants and stank up the place. From the looks on their faces, it had been a near thing. And the angel stink in this place was bad enough without adding more unpleasantness on top.

But Beelzebub stayed where he was. He crossed his arms. "Then the time has come. We fight for the throne of hell, and the command of Hell's forces."

As he spoke, his human guise melted away. He stood before me in his true form, skin blackened and cracked, with molten fire running underneath. The vestiges of his wings, cracked stumps of charred bone, spread out behind him.

"I never wanted this," he said, his blazing eyes sorrowful. "I would have used all the power at my command to serve you until the end of my days. But you have gone astray. You will face my full might as second-in-command of the Fallen. We will see if you can defeat me with whatever puny human weapon you brought to this fight."

The situation was even worse than Beelzebub imagined. More fool me, I hadn't even bothered to bring a weapon. After thousands of years of enduring the Fallen groveling at my feet, I had assumed the weight of my authority would be enough. Despite my earlier confrontation with Beelzebub, I had thought a stern look and a direct order would sway even him when the chips were down.

Besides, it wasn't like I kept any human weapons in my apartment. Didn't have much need for that kind of thing these days. And I had been in a bit of a hurry.

Uriel let out a strangled gasp. I had heard that sound from angels before, back in the war. Usually shortly after I impaled them on my blade, and shortly before they keeled over dead.

I didn't understand why his eyes went wide all of a sudden. Not until I felt my own skeletal wings extend out behind me. They brushed the walls to either side of the crappy apartment. I had no sensation left in what remained of my wings, but the soft impact jarred the bones and sent a shivery tremor through my back.

I looked down at my hands. The skin was cracked obsidian, with thick red lava visible through deep cracks. I didn't have to look in a mirror to know I was wearing my true face now. The face I hadn't worn since I had walked away from my throne centuries ago. And no wonder—I had forgotten how inconvenient this body was. I was as tall as an angel now; my head almost brushed the ceiling. I wouldn't be able to step through a doorway without ducking, and that wasn't even getting into the mechanics of how to maneuver my useless wings around in a space as small as this.

But that was just fine with me, because I wasn't planning on leaving through the door. If Beelzebub didn't leave right this instant, I intended to burn this place down around his ears.

"Did you forget why you and the rest of the Fallen put me in command in the first place?" My tone was conversational, but my voice still carried an echo of that unearthly thunder. "Or why you forced me onto that throne? Even before Hell corrupted you, you always valued raw strength too highly. And I was always the strongest of you."

I didn't try to look away from Uriel anymore. I stared down at his wide eyes, his mangled knee, the symbols carved into his bleeding arms. My body stretched taller until I had to duck just to keep from bashing my head on the ceiling. The black flames of corrupted power danced across my skin.

It looked like I had finally found something I cared about.

"Lord Lucifer..." Finally, too late, I heard real fear in Beelzebub's voice. "Lord Lucifer, please."

"The challenge begins now." My voice lowered to a growl, then rose to a shriek. Flames gouted from my mouth, leapt from my skin, shot out from my fingertips. They enveloped

Beelzebub until I couldn't see him anymore, only a towering bonfire of dark flame.

Once, they had called me Lightbringer. But that had been before the Fall. There was no light to be found in me anymore. But the strength... that was still mine.

Beelzebub had never even gotten the chance to attack.

I picked up Uriel, careful not to jar his broken places any more than I had to, and held him tightly against me. But I didn't need to bother. The fire didn't spread. It clung greedily to Beelzebub, until his screams died away and the smell of burning rancid meat almost covered up the smell of angel.

And here I had been sure I would end up burning the whole building down. It had been too long since I had used my power; I had forgotten how it worked. Apparently I was going to need to figure out how to get these inconvenient wings through a human doorway after all.

I watched the mound of flame that was Beelzebub writhe a little longer before I pursed my lips and blew the fire away. It died a little at a time, showering the room in purple sparks. Underneath, Beelzebub's blackened flesh had almost burned away, leaving him a mess of purply-red flesh and lava-like blood and sticky clear fluid. But he wasn't dead. His chest rose and fell, and with every exhale he let out a wheezing moan.

Good. That was what I had been hoping for. Not that I would have shed a tear if he had died. The empty, order-following automaton that had been Beelzebub for the last millennium bore no resemblance to the angel he had once been. I had seen a spark of his old self there at the end, when he had defied me, but not enough to deceive me into believing he was back. Times change, and time changes us all.

But while I knew I would never get my old friend back, I could still make use of what he had become.

He raised his head with what looked like a massive effort. His rolling eyes found mine. "You win," he gasped out. "The throne remains yours."

"No," I said. "I defeated you, which means you are mine to command. And my only command is this: take the throne of Hell. Bring order to my realm—your realm now—however you see fit. And never let me see your face again."

"Lord Lucifer... I..." His face cycled through several emotions, most of them various shades of confusion, before settling on relief. "I am eternally grateful for your mercy. I will serve you to the best of my—"

"Shut up." If I had to listen to one more word of his fawning, I would burn the place down after all. He had been proud once. "Get out of here. Before I change my mind and kill you."

"Yes, Lord Lucifer." He tried to rise to his feet, and collapsed. He tried again. Fell again. In the end, he crawled on bleeding, oozing legs out the door.

And left me standing in the middle of the bloodstained floor with a broken archangel cradled in my arms.

* * *

He didn't die, of course. It's not that easy to kill an angel—I would know, I've tried to kill enough of them. A few more hours, and he was good as new. He probably lost most of the blood that human shell had in it, though. I had a feeling he would be the one getting a written complaint from his landlord this time around.

I stayed with him until he healed up all the way. Seeing as how it was my subjects who had carved him up in the first place, it was the least I could do. Even if he didn't deserve it.

I wasn't sure he knew I was there. He was pretty out of it most of the time. He fell asleep after a while. After that, I sat with him long enough to watch his human body finish knitting itself back together, and then slipped out the door before he could wake up. I couldn't let him open his eyes to find Lucifer, lord of Hell—former lord of Hell—sitting by his bedside. Bad for my image, and all.

I wasn't even sure whether he'd been aware enough during that whole mess to remember who had saved him. I figured if he did, I would hear about it at our next chess game. Or not. Who even knew whether he would bother showing up anymore? He'd been enough of a no-show when he *hadn't* had an apocalyptic crisis to deal with.

But I woke up the next morning—all right, the next afternoon—to an insistent knocking at my door. After five minutes of pressing my pillow over my head and hoping the visitor would go away, I stumbled out of bed and opened the door to find Uriel standing in the hallway. He was still wearing his Onyx getup, even though by now he had to know he wasn't fooling anyone.

I blinked at him. And blinked again. He had never come to my apartment before. After a while, I had stopped inviting him. I hadn't even known he remembered the address.

"What are you doing here?" I finally asked—which, all right, wasn't the friendliest of greetings, but in my defense, I had just been rudely awakened.

"I came to thank you," said Onyx, with that flat, serious owl-stare of his. "For saving my life."

I didn't look him in the eye—I had learned my lesson last time—but that stare was unnerving enough even without meeting it straight-on. Honestly, I didn't know how he ever managed to pass for human.

"Oh. Right. So you remember that, then." I shifted from foot to foot, and wondered if I was supposed to invite him in.

"I remember." He let the silence stretch on just long enough to be awkward. Then he said, "If I'm remembering correctly, you enjoy human cuisine."

I blinked again at the change of subject, well aware that I had spent more than half this conversation blinking at him like a dummy. "You could say that."

"I'd like to share a meal with you at a human restaurant. To thank you for what you did for me." He flashed a rare, shy smile. "My treat."

I tugged at my ear. "I'm sorry, did I just hear you say you wanted to voluntarily spend time together? Doing something we didn't schedule beforehand?"

"This is how humans express gratitude, is it not?"

"I wouldn't know. Never been human." But I was already pulling on my coat. What can I say, I'm not one to turn down an opportunity for human cooking. Especially not on someone else's dime.

Which was how, half an hour later, I found myself sitting across from the Archangel Uriel at some hoity-toity French restaurant downtown. The kind of place where they don't print the prices on the menus. Where normally they don't even let you in the door if you're wearing jeans or a band t-shirt, or have the general stink of disreputability about you. I, by the way, was three for three. But however much Uriel slipped the maître d', it was enough to not only get us in the door, but let us skip the line even though we didn't have a reservation.

I'd had no idea Uriel had access to that kind of money. Even I didn't have pockets deep enough to afford this place, and I had the Prince of Greed on my payroll. I almost asked, but Uriel could be as skittish as a stray cat. I didn't want him running off on me.

"Reaching out to the Fallen was a boneheaded move," I said in lieu of a toast, as I raised my glass of overpriced red wine to my lips. It tasted the same as the box wine I normally bought, but then, I was no connoisseur. At least not when it came to wines. Baked goods were a different story.

"We take our allies where we can find them," Uriel replied, as expressionless as he ever was over the chess table.

"Yeah, well, the part you neglected to take into account was that the Fallen are all idiots." I paused, frowned, and corrected myself. "Well, most of them. The rest are brilliant, which is worse."

Uriel swirled his own wine in his glass. He sniffed appreciatively, then took a tiny sip and rolled it around in his mouth. He closed his eyes and smiled. But by the time he set the glass down, the smile had disappeared.

"What are you going to do now? More of the same, I take it?" He said the words in such an aggressively flat tone that it was impossible to tell whether he meant them as an insult or not. With anyone else, I would have said yes... but, well, this was Uriel.

I opened my mouth, then realized I didn't know how to answer. Truth was, there was nothing I would have liked more than to hole up in my apartment, bake a double batch of all fifty Christmas-cookie recipes, and stuff a cookie in my mouth every time I was tempted to think about what came next for Heaven and Hell. And worse, what it would mean for my cozy existence here on Earth.

And technically speaking, there was nothing preventing me from doing just that. I had even managed to rid myself of my throne. I was a free agent now, and could do as I pleased without anyone bowing at my feet or pestering me for orders.

But change was coming, whether I liked it or not. And if I thought it wouldn't show up at my door just because I didn't go looking for it... well, then I was just asking for a rude awakening.

Going back to Hell was out of the question. I had burned that bridge, and I had no regrets. But if sitting on my throne and commanding my old army wasn't an option, and neither was locking myself in my apartment for a good long baking binge, then where did that leave me?

I eyed Uriel speculatively. Hadn't he been looking for a partner, someone to keep the worst of the consequences from spilling over onto the human world? I'd never had any desire to emulate Uriel's do-gooder lifestyle. Just because he felt guilty for taking the wrong side when it really counted, that didn't make it my problem. I had already done my part. I had fought the good fight. As far as I was concerned, I had earned a few millennia to lick my wounds.

But if laziness, denial, and gluttony were all off the table... well, what else was I going to do with my time?

The problem was, making that suggestion to Uriel would amount to asking the archangel for his help—and I was the Prince of Pride, for Hell's sake. I tipped half the contents of my wineglass into my mouth to buy myself time to figure out what to say. Uriel shot me a disapproving frown across the table. This must have been the kind of wine that was too expensive to gulp—which made it not worth the money, as far as I was concerned.

I set my glass down. Cleared my throat. "Alliances between angels and demons are a bad idea to begin with," I said gruffly. I wasn't sure whether I was trying to talk him into this, or talk myself out of it. "Almost as bad an idea as getting involved in this mess at all."

Uriel answered with a nod. "Yes. I learned that lesson the hard way. It's past time I stopped letting myself get complacent, and started remembering that the Fallen are the enemy."

I poured the rest of the wine into my mouth.

"No more fraternizing with the forces of Hell," Uriel continued. "Which, I'm afraid, means no more chess games. I apologize—it's nothing personal."

"Nope," I muttered, so quietly I wasn't sure Uriel could hear me. "It's just that I'm Fallen, which makes me the enemy. Not personal at all."

"I don't think I'll be around much from now on, anyway," said Uriel. "I have work to do, and I can't do it from down here. It's time for me to end my self-imposed exile, return home, and take this opportunity to reform Heaven from within."

"Let me know how that works out for you." I hated to sound so cynical, but, well... been there, done that.

"I think my attempted alliance with the Fallen was only an excuse to keep from having to go back. Our work together would by necessity have been limited to Earth, since the Fallen can't enter Heaven without an angel feather, and I have no intention of handing those out to the forces of Hell."

"Of course not. Seeing as we're the enemy, and all. But, you know. Nothing personal." Maybe I sounded a little bitter. But Uriel *had* kind of pulled the rug out from under me there. I could hardly go and make him my offer now.

I eyed my empty wine glass, and wondered if Uriel would take it askance if I went ahead and drained his too. Probably. With a sigh, I resisted the temptation. "This little dinner was never really about saying thanks, was it? It was about saying goodbye."

"You've been a good friend to me over the centuries. I think perhaps I haven't said that enough."

I was pretty sure he had never said it at all. "It's all right. Some people say they care with a Hallmark card, some people say it by glaring silently over a chessboard." I blinked back a sudden wetness in my eyes. It was a good thing none of my subjects—former subjects—were here to see me now. I had a reputation to uphold, after all. Just because I was no longer sitting on the throne of Hell, that didn't mean I was ready to become the laughingstock of the place.

"I let you win most of those games, you know."

"Yeah, I figured that out pretty quick." I had never suspected. If Uriel weren't so maddeningly honest, I would have assumed he was lying.

"Goodbye, Lucifer. May our paths cross again." Uriel rose from his chair.

"Wait, you're leaving already? We haven't even ordered yet." What kind of sneaky bait-and-switch was this? Was the thought of sitting across the table from me for more than five minutes without a chessboard between us that intolerable?

"I... am finding this unexpectedly difficult. I think it would be best for me to leave as soon as possible." He blinked too fast. His eyes shone too brightly. "Order whatever you like. I've taken care of the bill."

I didn't think I could have eaten a bite if I had been starving to death. The dancing fish had returned to my stomach, and they had brought friends. Only they weren't dancing anymore; they had moved on to karate practice. "Are you sure going back is worth it? Take it from me, turning that place around will be harder than it looks. You know Michael will be gunning for the throne, and he plays dirty."

"I am prepared to give my life, if it is required." He blinked harder. "I... I need to leave."

Oh, so he thought he could go and get himself killed like it was nothing, was that it? Selfish bastard, just like always. He didn't even bother to think about the fact that without him, I had no one. I didn't even have a decent plan for the future, not if he was going to go all *the Fallen are the enemy* on me. What was I supposed to do, figure out this do-gooder thing on my own?

"I have something for you. A parting gift." He dug around in his pocket, and pulled something out in his clenched fist. "Thank you again. For everything."

He opened his hand. Something small and white fluttered to the table.

By the time I stopped staring and picked my jaw up off the floor, Uriel was gone.

I snatched up Uriel's gift and hurried out of the restaurant. "Uriel!" I didn't care who heard me, or what name he wanted me to use. "You can't do something like that and then just leave! Get back here!"

But when I pushed the door open, and looked down the sidewalk both ways, Uriel was gone.

I opened my hand and stared down at the angel feather. He couldn't have just given Lucifer the Lightbringer, dread commander of the Fallen, a get-out-of-Hell-free card. Not my friend the the duty-bound archangel with a stick up his ass a mile long. Not cowardly Uriel, who was all for supporting the cause right up until it meant putting his own neck on the line.

He couldn't have.

He had.

I could free myself from the shackles of Hell. From the ache of despair. The hollow emptiness. The burning. I couldn't remember what it was like not to burn.

I could walk the golden streets of Heaven again.

And then what? This didn't exactly make it any easier to answer my questions about the future. If anything, the questions had just multiplied.

With nothing tying me to Hell, and no way for my former subjects to pull me back into their drama against their will, maybe I really could to live that quiet life I dreamed of. Or I could go back to Heaven, take a stroll down the old familiar streets, get used to the smell of angel. I could make my own bid for the throne—with Heaven's forces in disarray, my chances would be better than last time, even without my army behind me. If nothing else, maybe I could stop Uriel from making whatever senseless self-sacrificing gesture he had planned.

Or maybe, now that Uriel was gone, it was time for someone else to pick up where he had left off. Shield the humans from the fallout of whatever schemes both sides were about to put in motion. Protect those widows and orphans. Do what I could, where I could, to hold the end of the world at bay.

Yes, I was talking about me. Who else was going to bother? It wasn't like Beelzebub was going to do it.

I tucked the feather into my pocket. I was going to use it, of course. And then I would figure out where to go from there. But... not just yet. For now, I would go for a walk. Maybe whip up a batch of cookies. Sit down and eat with my old friends loneliness and despair. They were the only friends I had left. I wasn't ready to say goodbye just yet.

I turned toward my apartment, already flipping through recipes in my head. Today was a chocolate chip kind of day.

UP NEXT

When human justice fails, the desperate call me.

You know things are bad when a fallen angel is one of the good guys. Only I'm not much more than human myself now. Not since I lost my magic in the war that defeated the big boss in Heaven for good.

I stay away from the supernatural these days. I've got enough regular old human wrongs to right without borrowing trouble I no longer have the firepower to handle. That rule worked great until today. Now there's a beautiful woman on my doorstep with a demon problem. She doesn't stand a chance on her own. But if I let her in, it's only a matter of time before this job brings me face to face with the secret I've worked so hard to leave behind.

Get **Righteous Devil** at your favorite bookstore,
or online at https://www.zjcannon.com

WANT MORE?

Subscribe to Z.J. Cannon's weekly news and updates at https://www.zjcannon.com/newsletter to find out the second a new book comes out, get sneak peeks and opportunities to read upcoming releases early, and find out what projects are in the works. Plus, dog pictures! When you sign up, you'll get a free electronic copy of *No Regrets*, an exclusive introduction to the Iron Bound urban fantasy series.

ABOUT THE AUTHOR

Cruelty, selfishness, greed... this world is full of darkness. But light still exists, caged but undimmed, an unquenchable spark at the core of the human heart. And that spark is worth fighting for.

Some people are still willing to fight. Bloodied and broken, they rise undaunted from every defeat to fight for justice and compassion in a world that has none. But before they can drive back the world's darkness, they'll need to confront the darkness in their own souls.

These are the heroes at the heart of Z.J. Cannon's work, which blends page-turning suspense with high-stakes drama to create stories about flawed and often deeply damaged people fighting against overwhelming odds to do what's right.

Also by Z.J. Cannon

Nic Ward
Nothing Sacred
Broken Faith
Crooked Idols
Lost Cause
Blood Sacrament
Fallen Saints
Blighted Angels
Sinners' Kingdom
Righteous Devil

Hound of Hades
Death Trace
Memory Game
Ghost Town
Night Terrors
Hell Bent
Blind Side
Trinity Gambit
Friendly Fire
Bitter Fruit
Skeleton Key
Hound of Hades: The Short Stories

Iron Bound
No Promises
No Illusions
No Sanctuary
No Escape
No Heroes